Little Boy Blue

Margaret Fenton

Aakenbaaken & Kent

ISBN: 9781958022184

Dedication

This book is dedicated to:
Judith Claire Herring
1943-1989
The best mother ever,
and
John Stephen Herring
1972-2022
The best brother ever.
I miss you both.
Rest in Peace

Chapter One

"Please, Claire?"

"No."

"Please?"

"No, LaReesa."

"Please?"

This time I sang it, to the tune of "La Cucaracha," "No no no no no no no no, no no no no no."

Reese scowled at me. "Yo voice sucks."

I laughed. "Thanks!"

LaReesa Jones was my thirteen-year-old foster child. Being a single foster parent to a black teenage girl was not easy. Things were easier when Grant Summerville was living with me. Grant had been my boyfriend, and I, in a moment of total stupidity, had cheated on him with a friend of mine named Kirk Mahoney. Grant discovered my mistake, ended our relationship, and moved out of my house. I hadn't seen or heard from Grant since January, and it was now June. I missed him. The tears that lingered in the back of my eyes threatened to well again. I blinked them back.

Kirk was gone, too. *The Birmingham News* had been absorbed by a digital media corporation that had discontinued the print newspaper altogether. Most of the reporters had been let go, but Kirk was kept on and assigned to cover the state legislature down in Montgomery. I read his articles sometimes online. Stories about what bills were introduced and by whom. What passed. What didn't. I suspected he was chewing his arm off due to boredom.

"Papa Doc said he'd buy me one," LaReesa continued.

Papa Doc was her nickname for my father, Dr. Christopher Conover, and we were in the car on our way to his house now. He was a retired psychotherapist and had, in a saintly way, stepped up and volunteered to watch Reese during the summer months while she was out of school and I worked as a child welfare social worker for the Jefferson County Department of Human Services. Dad was cleaning out forty years of extra stuff from his house on the bluff with LaReesa's help, and it seemed, so far, to be keeping her occupied. LaReesa's mother, Amara Jones, was a prostitute and a drug addict. She was recently out of prison. Keeping Reese out of that way of life was proving to be a struggle.

I scanned the dashboard of my over-a-decade-old Honda Civic. "Papa Doc needs to buy me a car, first." I muttered. I turned the Honda into the driveway of my father's house. "Look, LaReesa, you are only thirteen, almost fourteen, years old. You are over two years away from getting a driver's license. After that happens, we can talk about cars."

She exited the car, tossing her long black braids over her shoulder and slamming the car door without a word as my father emerged from the front door of the tan brick, ranch-style house where I had grown up. Dad's long hair had once been blonde like mine but was now mostly gray. It was pulled into a ponytail, which revealed the white crescent-shaped scar on his left cheek he had gotten from the police while helping in the struggle for civil rights.

Reese stormed past him as he walked to the driveway. I rolled down my window and greeted him. The day was going to be a hot one. A puff of warm humid air blew into my face as the window rolled down.

"Good Tuesday morning, Claire. I see we are in a mood today."

"Lately it's every day. Did you tell her you'd buy her a car?"

"I said when the time comes, we'd talk about it. She's a long way from sixteen."

"It's all she can talk about, so I'm afraid you are going to hear a lot about it."

"It's okay. I have experience with difficult teenage behavior."

I hung my head. I had been awful to my father when I was thirteen. Angry and grieving my mother, who died of breast cancer that year. "Yeah, sorry."

He smiled. "I'm kidding. You seem to have turned out all right. I'm proud of you, and I hope you have a good day."

I put the car in reverse. "You, too, and thanks again for watching her."

I headed down Shades Mountain on Oxmoor Road, then

to I-65 north where I joined the slow vehicle crawl to work. I pulled into the parking lot behind our building downtown and was in my cubicle-office by ten after eight. Russell, my office mate, joined me five minutes later. We greeted each other.

"How's Reese?"

"She's almost fourteen. Snaps at me constantly."

"Normal, then. Any word from her mamma?"

LaReesa's mother had been released from the Julia Tutwiler Prison for Women in Wetumpka in March. She had sent Reese a couple of letters about how she was going to get custody of her back. I had explained to Reese, who had explained to her mother in several letters, that she was in the custody of the State of Alabama and Amara would have to file for custody with the Court. And pass drug tests. The letters had stopped, and my checks with our social worker and Family Court told me she had yet to file anything. I hoped she never would.

"No word. Hope it stays that way."

"Probably will. You got a busy day?" Russell asked.

"Not so far." The end of the school year always slowed us down a little. "You?"

"I'm going to go out and check on Reese's cousins this afternoon, I think, before I finally transfer them to the Foster-Adoptive Unit."

"Let me know how they are doing." LaReesa's three young cousins had come into foster care late last year because her aunt was also in prison and her grandmother, who had custody, died. From all accounts, they were flourishing where they were.

Russell and I worked in the office, back-to-back, at our desks until mid-morning. Then Jessica, our despicable unit secretary, appeared in the doorway.

"Russell, Mac wants to see you. Dr. Pope's in there, too."

Russell shot me a look. Mac McAlister was our Unit Supervisor. A summons from Mac wasn't terribly unusual. I just hoped it wasn't a problem with one of Russell's cases. Dr. Teresa Pope was the County Director, and a summons from her was very unusual. Both of us were curious as he made his way toward Mac's office, on the perimeter of our floor.

He was gone a long time. I was starting to worry about him and wondering what was up when Mac appeared in the door. Mac was a pudgy man with a ring of gray hair whose loose tie was always too short. He pointed at me with his ever-present unlit cigar. "My office."

I followed him through the maze of cubicles to his office, where rust-colored files from our unit were stacked everywhere, waiting on reviews. Dr. Pope sat in one of the chairs facing Mac's desk. Everything about her was perfect, as usual. Her hair, her posture, her suit. I straightened my wrinkled shirt as I looked at Russell, who stood near the window, a serious look on his handsome, blond-hair-framed face. Mac motioned toward the remaining unoccupied chair in front of his desk. "Sit."

I sat, as directed. Mac looked at me. "We have been discussing whether or not we should even share this with you."

"What?" I asked. My mind was racing.

Mac continued. "We received a report this morning. I am assigning this to Russell. You are not, *not*, to get involved with this case in any way. I want that to be very clear." Next to me, Dr. Pope nodded.

I took the single sheet of white paper he offered me. It was a reporting form, the first step that happens when someone calls in a report of child abuse or neglect. The social worker in the intake unit takes all the information and gives it to Mac, who assigns it to one of us.

Name of complainant, it said. "Regina Maynard" was written in loopy handwriting. Name of child, Dylan Maynard. Age 6. Male.

Name of the accused, Grant Summerville.

Chapter Two

"Oh, *hell* no!"

I stood up and paced the room. "That bitch. Absolutely not." I could feel the hot rage as it started in my chest and radiated outward. "She stole from him, Mac! Stole money from a lot of his clients. He pressed charges. Had her arrested. She's just pissed. You can't believe that he would…" My voice trailed off as I scanned the rest of the form.

Regina had been an employee of my ex-boyfriend until January of this year, six months ago. Now she claimed her son, Dylan, told her that on the days when she brought him to High Tech, he had been alone with Grant in the bathroom and Grant had touched his private parts. Then Grant made Dylan touch him. I could feel my face starting to burn. "This is *bullshit*. Grant is not a child molester. Never."

Dr. Pope interceded. "Claire, we are assigning this to Russell. He is going to do a thorough evaluation and likely refer Dylan to The Cole Center to get further info. We'll get to the bottom of this."

"Does Grant know, yet?"

Russell said, "I just got the case. I'm going to call him in."

"I want to be there."

Mac said, "What did I *just* say? You are *absolutely not* to have anything to do with this case. I'm not kidding."

"I agree," Dr. Pope said. "You are way too involved emotionally to be part of this."

Russell added, "I know you love him, Claire. I'll get to the bottom of this. I promise."

My rage wasn't abating, and I was nearly shouting. "He was *never* alone with Dylan in the bathroom. Dylan is six! He's able to go to the bathroom on his own. Grant would *not* follow a child in there! She's just mad because she got caught stealing. She's a crook and she is trying to take him down with her. God damn her!"

Russell approached me and wrapped his arms around me in a warm hug. "Deep breath," he whispered in my ear. "Trust me."

I followed his advice and inhaled deeply. Then again. The tears were back, suddenly, and I wiped my eyes with my fingers. I always cry when I am furious, and I hate that. I didn't want to fall apart in front of Dr. Pope and Mac.

"Claire, we are going to watch this case carefully, I promise." Dr. Pope said. "Please trust us."

I nodded, still blinking back tears. "I have to get back to work."

Russell followed me back to our office. When we reached there, I asked, "Do you have Grant's cell number?"

He glanced at the paper in his hand and read a number. "Is that it?"

"That's it."

"I'm going to call him now, see if he can come in this afternoon. By the way, Mac and Dr. Pope didn't want to tell you about this. I convinced them it would be worse if you heard it through the office grapevine, so to speak."

"True. Thank you. What else did they say?"

"That I am to approach this investigation with an open mind and no preconceived notions."

"Do they know you've spent time with Grant?"

"I didn't share that information with them, so I don't think so. I don't want this going to someone else, and I'm next on the assignment rotation, anyway."

"Thank you. I'm grateful."

"You have to stay out of my way, though. Promise?"

"Of course."

"God, Claire, you can't lie."

He was right. "I'll do my best."

He picked up the phone on his desk and dialed Grant's number. I tried to focus on the update for a client on my desk, but I couldn't help but overhear Russell's half of the conversation.

"Hi, Grant. I don't know if you remember me. Russell DePaul? Claire Conover's coworker from DHS? Yeah, well, we've got a situation here. There's been a report made against you…. I don't want to go into too much detail over the phone. Can you come to the office this afternoon? …Sure, that's fine. See you then."

Russell hung up the phone, then turned around and looked at me. "He'll be here at four. I need to go reserve us a room." He left the cubicle.

I checked my schedule on my phone. I didn't have anything at four today. I was going to be here. For sure.

The day crawled by. I wrote a court report, then re-wrote it. I spent some time on the phone trying to find an affordable day care spot for one of my toddler clients. Mostly I just stared at the wall.

Four o'clock rolled around, and Russell got a call from Nancy at the front desk that Grant was here. He thanked her and stood up. So did I.

"No! No, Claire. Let me do this first. I don't want his seeing you to throw him off."

"He probably hates me. I just want to say hi."

"No. Please, come find us after. We'll be in the third-floor conference room."

Russell picked up a notepad and left. I gave him a ten-minute head start while I brushed my hair and fixed my makeup, then walked upstairs. The conference room was in the middle of the floor. Its walls were made of glass so whoever was in there was visible. I paused in the hallway and peeked into the room.

Russell had his back to me, facing Grant across the long table. My heart skipped a beat when I saw him. He'd cut his hair a little shorter, I noted, the loose, brown curls were less in his face than before. His thin, six-foot-five frame was dressed in a navy-blue polo shirt with the High Tech logo on the breast, and khaki pants. I remembered with a smile that he always wore khaki pants. He had like twenty pairs of them of all different shades in his closet. He wore the same glasses I remembered, with black plastic frames. He looked good. Damn good.

Russell was talking and I watched as the color drained out of Grant's face. Grant had a way of remaining calm in the face of just about anything. I was the one who screamed and shouted, and got animated when we had argued, which was rarely. Russell kept talking, asking questions which Grant answered. After about fifteen minutes, they both stood up. I went and stood by the door to the room.

Russell exited first, giving me an exasperated look when he saw me. Grant came out of the door, and I said, "Hi."

"Hi. I was wondering if you were here."

"Of course. How are you?"

"Fine."

"Good."

Russell said, "Claire, would you mind walking him out?"

"Yeah, I can do that."

I led him to the elevator and we entered. I pushed the button for the first floor and he asked, "Do you know why I'm here?"

"I do. Damn that Regina. I have been told to have nothing to do with this case. Russell will handle it. You are in good hands."

"I know. How's Kirk?"

"I don't know. He moved to Montgomery six months ago, and I haven't talked to him. Don't want to, either."

"How is LaReesa? She still with you?"

"She's great. She's with Dad for the summer days, helping him get his house cleared out. She passed all her classes, even math, and will go to ninth grade in the fall."

"Awesome. I was worried about that math grade."

"Me, too."

His voice caught a bit when he asked the next question. "So," he cleared his throat. "Are you seeing anybody?"

No, I'm not over you, I thought. *I miss you. I love you.*

"No. You?"

"No. Work is keeping me busy. And all this crap with Regina."

The elevator door opened to the first floor and my friends at the front desk, Beth and Nancy, waved to us. "Where did you park?"

"In the back lot."

I headed toward the back door, happy that this route would give us more time to talk. "What's going on with the case against Regina?"

"I got notified that we are going to court in August. She's

pled not guilty. I can't believe she's filed this report against me."

"It's false, and Russell will prove that."

"I hope so."

He opened the back door for me and I walked him as far as his van. The High Tech logo shone bright in royal blue and lime green on the white door. "Call me if you have questions, okay? I mean, I'm not working this case, but if you have questions about how things work in the system, I can answer them. If you don't hate me," I added.

He reached over and picked up the ends of my light blonde hair on my left shoulder, stroking them between his fingers. He used to do that, sometimes, when we were together. "I don't hate you," he muttered. "I couldn't hate you."

"You don't have to," I said. "Because I hate myself."

I picked Reese up at five-thirty from Dad's. I went in the house and he offered me a glass of lemonade, which sounded fantastic. He poured me one from the pitcher in the fridge and we stood in the kitchen and talked. Dad said Reese was in the bathroom.

Dad had not changed anything in the house since my mother died all those years ago. She had picked out the floral valance curtains that hung over the window above the sink. I fidgeted as I stared out of the window.

"What's up?"

"What do you mean?"

"You are super keyed up. Anxious about something."

"Bad day at work."

"You wanna talk about it?"

"You remember all that stuff that happened with Grant's employee, Regina Maynard, right before we broke up?"

"She was the one that stole from him and his clients?"

"Right. She's made a report against him, alleging sexual abuse against her son. Grant came to the office today."

LaReesa burst into the kitchen from the living room. "That fucking bitch!"

"Language, LaReesa!" I snapped.

15

"But she is!"

"No doubt. But that language from a thirteen-year-old sounds trashy."

"Did you see him? Did you see Grant? How is he?" she asked.

I held my hands up in front of me. "Whoa. One at a time. Yes, I saw him. He looks great. He's lost a little weight and gotten a haircut, but he looks good. He asked about you, and said he was proud of you for passing math."

"Let's beat her down."

"What?"

"Go find this…beyotch…and beat her down. Get her to admit she lied."

My dad asked, "Do you really think that's the best way to handle this? What would be the consequences if you got caught?"

Good point, Dad, I thought. Help Reese to develop some logic skills by thinking about her actions. I raised my eyebrows at her. "Well?"

"Ain't nobody gonna find out. It's what the cops do, anyway."

"Really?" I asked her.

"Y'all ain't never lived on the streets, and it shows."

We laughed and I put my arm around her shoulders. "Let's go home."

We bid dad goodbye and headed for the car. As we drove home, I realized that maybe LaReesa was right. Not about the beatdown, of course, but maybe it was time to go on the offensive.

Chapter Three

Reese and I got home and talked about dinner. She had developed an interest in cooking lately and began to prepare a chicken casserole for us to eat. While she did that, I changed into comfy clothes, went into my office, and called Grant.

"Hey," he answered.

"Hey, you busy?"

"No, I just got home. What's up?"

"I had a thought. Maybe we should gather some information about Regina."

"Why?"

I thought for a second. "To, I don't know, show her motive in this? I feel totally blindsided and powerless."

"I do too."

"Do you have a list of the clients she stole from, in addition to you?"

"Yeah, of course. It has taken me the majority of the past six months to put it all together, with the help of an investigator from an attorney's office. Hang on, I gotta get on my laptop."

A few moments later, he read me a list of five businesses that I wrote down on a notepad. He had the totals, too. Regina had allegedly stolen some cash from some individual people, and they had filed those charges separately with the police department. It was a lot. The grand total of everything was $8,846. Grant agreed to send me her resume and any background he had on her.

Grant continued, "And I have no idea why she would do this. I paid her a fair salary. She had enough for her rent and everything. I taught her a skill. I'm just bowled over."

"Does she have a drug problem?"

"Not that I know of. She passed her drug tests for me."

"I want to go and get some background information on her. Like I said, maybe if we had some information, we could put together some sort of explanation, or defense. Something."

"How is Reese?"

"She has developed an interest in cooking and baking lately. It's been fun. We've had a lot of cupcakes, so I my waistline is getting bigger."

"Sounds yummy."

"You should come over for dinner sometime soon. Let her make you something. She'd love to see you."

There was a long moment of silence and I wondered if I'd pushed it too far. I held my breath.

"Yeah, I think I'd like that. When?"

"Friday?"

"What time?"

"Five? Come have drinks and dinner?"

"I'll see you then."

I hung up the cell phone, and I had butterflies in my stomach. I went to the kitchen, where Reese was putting the casserole dish in the oven.

"Guess who I was talking to?"

"Who?"

"Grant. He's coming over for dinner on Friday. I was hoping you could make him something."

That earned me a big gap-toothed smile. "Awesome! He likes Italian food. I found a recipe for chicken marsala that I want to try, if you'll get the wine."

"I will."

"I can't wait to see him."

I took a big breath. "Me neither."

I checked my email after Reese and I had dinner, and there was one from GSummerville@hightech.com. I opened it and it was a short note. *Hey, attached please find what you requested. See you Friday, G.*

Attached as a word .doc was a resume. I opened it. Regina Renee Maynard was printed in a fancy font at the top. Birthdate was next, September 19, twenty-three years ago. Wow, she'd had Dylan at age seventeen. That was young. She'd still been in high school. She'd withdrawn from Blount County High School when she was eighteen. That was the end of the education section of her resume.

Blount County was the county immediately north of us here in Jefferson County. I was glad she was from there instead of here. It meant I could sneak up there one day soon and do some investigating. I didn't know anyone up there, which hopefully meant no one knew me.

Her work experience was listed next. She'd done a short stint as a cashier at a Dollar General in Hayden, one of the towns up there. After that she'd gotten a job as a secretary for a title company, again in Hayden. Then she was out of work for a while. I supposed that she still lived with her parents at that point and they supported her. Next, she had a job at a mom-and-pop restaurant, waiting tables. That didn't last long at all, only about three months. I wondered who was watching baby Dylan when she was working all these jobs. I'd guess her parents.

After the restaurant was some time at a cell phone store. Again, she left after three months. There was another period of unemployment, then she turned up at a day care. Lord, by that time she was only twenty-two. She'd had five jobs in two years. I wondered what in the hell had made Grant hire her. I knew, though. He was a big, soft-hearted guy. The story of a single mom struggling would have convinced him.

High Tech was next, though it wasn't listed on the C.V. He'd hired her in the late summer of last year, a couple of months after we met. I remembered how fast his company had grown during that time. He almost had more clients than he could keep up with, and was glad to find anyone to work. I was working the Samantha Chambless case then, and had just met LaReesa. I didn't remember his talking about Regina much. Then again, I thought with a twinge of guilt, I hadn't been paying much attention. I saved the resume and closed my laptop.

I walked into the living room. LaReesa lay in a chair, sideways, her legs propped over the armrest. She typed with her thumbs on her phone as the TV played some mindless reality show. I needed to go do the dishes, instead I collapsed on the couch.

LaReesa glanced at me and asked, "What?"

"Nothing. I can't just sit here?"

She shrugged. "You do you. I'm looking at recipes. Tryin' to decide what to make Friday with the marsala. What do you think?"

"A salad is always good with pasta. Shall we go shopping Thursday?"

"That works."

I thought for a while about my day tomorrow. I checked my schedule on my cell phone. I didn't have Court until Monday, and everything on there could be rescheduled. I emailed Jessica the secretary that I was going to take a personal day. I needed some time off. As I sent the email, I thought for sure that Mac would clue in to what I was doing. I never took a random day off. I half-expected a phone call in the morning.

Wednesday morning came and went with no phone call, which I took as a good sign. I took Reese to Dad's, as usual. I didn't tell her I was going to be off work. After I dropped her off, I took I-65 north to Blount County. I exited the interstate and decided to start with the high school. I typed the address into my GPS and was there within minutes.

The school was huge, a two-story temple of learning that had been constructed in the last decade or so. I wondered if anyone would be here, since it was the summer holidays. Principals in Alabama are twelve-month employees, so someone should be here, I thought. The enormous double doors were unlocked, the security station unmanned. I made my way to the office.

The large room was empty, the long counter cleared and the lights off. I could see the lights on in one of the offices on the other side of the room. "Hello?" I called.

"Hello?" I woman's voice answered. "Hang on a second."

I waited, and within a minute an older woman appeared, short gray hair combed neatly and dressed in a red t-shirt tucked into jeans. She greeted me, her glance going to my work badge on the lanyard around my neck. I'd put it on this morning, as I always did, as I walked out of the door. The lanyard was bright blue, with JCDHS printed in yellow along it and therefore clearly showed my place of employment. I'd considered taking it off in the car, but I hoped it would lend my presence some authority.

"Can I help you?"

I smiled. "Hi, I'm Claire Conover, and I'm looking into something." I left it vague on purpose. "Are you the principal here?"

"I am. I'm Dr. Grace Allen."

"Do you have a second to talk?"

"I do."

I followed her to her office. The room was lined with bookcases, all sporting titles related to education. "School Leadership that Works", read one title. "Motivating Students Who Don't Care", read another. Her desk held a laptop and several piles of paper. I sat in the chair in front of her desk.

"How can I help you?"

"I'm trying to find information on one of your students from a few years ago."

"I was probably the assistant principal then. Who are you asking about?"

"Regina Maynard? She would have been here maybe five years ago?"

"Oh, Regina. Yes, I knew her." She sounded disappointed already.

"What can you tell me about her?"

"She was a below-average student. Not a behavior problem, really, just not very motivated to do well or go to college. Or graduate, for that matter. She dropped out after she had a baby. I met with her parents, who were both very nice, but not very educated themselves, so they didn't put much of an emphasis on it. You know what I mean?"

I did. That situation wasn't terribly uncommon here, no matter which county. "I do. She had the baby, I think, when she was seventeen?"

"She did. The birth kept her out of school, on a homeschool program, for about a month."

"Do you know who the father is?"

"She was dating Jerry Cook at the time, so I assume it's him. That relationship didn't last all that long, though. I've wondered how she is doing."

I ignored that. I wrote Jerry's name down in my cell phone. I wondered if she had named this Jerry on the birth certificate. I'd have to check when I got back to the office.

Russell should have pulled Dylan's birth certificate already. "Can you tell me anything else about her?"

"Not really. Her mother watched the baby on school days while she was in school until she quit. I think she had a boy, but I don't remember his name. I don't know what happened to her after that. Has she abused her son? Is she in trouble with DHS?" She nodded toward my badge.

I plastered on a smile. "I'm sorry; I really can't talk about it. It's confidential."

"Oh, okay. I wish her well, if you see her."

"Thank you for your time." I walked back to my car under the suspicious gaze of Dr. Allen. She was not a dumb lady, but I hoped she would forget I was ever there.

Chapter Four

I sped out of the parking lot of the high school and stopped in the parking lot of a gas station down the street. This morning, I had printed out a copy of the resume Grant had sent me and checked the piece of paper when I stopped. I decided to go to her first place of employment. Might as well do this in order.

I found the Dollar General in Hayden without any trouble. All the staff there were young, and none had worked there when Regina did, five years ago. The turnover in the store was unreal. The young manager offered to put in me in contact with someone from HR, but I declined. I sat in my car and thought about what to do next. It was nearly eleven a.m., and I wondered if the local restaurant Regina had worked in was still in business and if they served lunch. I typed the address into my phone and headed that way.

Grandma's Apron was old. The building looked as if it had been built about the same time as Hayden itself. It sat on the right side of the busy highway, dirty white paint covering a building that appeared to be constructed out of cinderblocks. The sign was cute, sporting a painting of a ruffled, floral pink and green apron with the name of the restaurant on it. One car, other than mine, sat in the parking lot.

I opened the glass door and walked in. A hostess station made of scratched oak was planted in front of the door. There was a faded, threadbare rug on the tile floor and the whole place had a stench of old fried food. The woman manning the station looked to be in her late seventies, her white hair neatly formed into curls on her head that needed to be combed out. To my left, I could see a middle-aged man sweeping the tile floor in the dining room.

"Can I help you?"

"Do you have food to go?"

"Yes, of course. Here's our menu." She handed me a greasy, plastic-laminated sheet. "Our chicken fingers are particularly tasty."

I was not going to think about the state of the fryer oil in that kitchen. "I think I want something lighter. Do you have sandwiches?"

"On the back, Sweetie."

I smiled. I love little old southern ladies who call everyone Sweetie. I flipped the sheet and ordered a turkey sandwich with chips, on toast. She wrote the order on a notepad and took it to the kitchen while I waited. No one walked in the door while she was gone.

When she returned, I asked, "I have some questions about someone who used to work here, five years ago? Would you be able to answer those, or is there a manager around?"

She straightened up and proudly declared, "My husband and I have owned this place for over forty years. I am the manager. Who are you asking about?"

"Regina Maynard?"

"Oh, Regina." Disappointment in her voice, too, just like the principal at the high school. "Is she in trouble? Did she hurt her baby?" The disappointment flipped to anxiety.

"No, no, I'm only trying to get some background information on her. What can you tell me?"

"Well," she sighed. "She worked here right after she dropped out of high school. We tried to work with her, since she had the new baby and all, but in the end, I had to let her go."

"How come?"

"Oh, she stole, Sweetie."

"Oh, no."

She nodded. "Yes, she stole credit card numbers from our patrons. Hurt the business, too. Hurt our reputation."

"I'm so sorry."

"You can order things online with just a credit card number, and that's what she did. Our customers would call and say they were getting notices of suspicious transactions. After about four of those calls, we started watching everyone. She was writing down the card numbers when she rung them up."

So Regina had been stealing for a while. "I'm so sorry. What an inconvenience. Did you press charges?"

"We thought about it, but she was just a kid. With a new baby, too. I thought about trying to work with her. If she'd just shown any remorse, you know? Some sense that she knew she had done wrong and would apologize. But she didn't."

A pudgy, older man with gray hair in a stained white t-shirt under an apron emerged from the back with a Styrofoam case in his hand, which he handed to me. I thanked him. "This is my husband, Fred Maple. He does the cooking here, and I wait on tables and host. I'm Henrietta Maple." She nodded toward the man in the dining area. "That's our son, Caleb."

"Nice to meet you." I balanced the sandwich on the host stand while I dug out my wallet. I paid for the sandwich with cash and left a large tip. I felt sorry for Henrietta and Fred, trying to make this restaurant work when clearly it wasn't. I thanked them again and made my way to my car. I sat there for a few minutes, rereading Regina's resume and trying to decide where to go next. There were still a couple of local places she had worked I wanted check out. The cell phone company, for sure. I took a bite of the turkey sandwich and noted it was dry and tasteless, without any condiments on it.

I was still thinking about my next move when my cell phone rang, and it was the office. I answered it. "Hello?"

Mac. "I need you at the office, right now."

"Is everything okay?"

"Right now!" He shouted, and hung up the phone on me.

Uh oh. I put the car in gear and headed for I-65 South. Within forty minutes I was in the back parking lot, and after throwing away the remains of the dry turkey sandwich, made my way to Mac's office on the second floor. Jessica sat at her desk outside, giving me a sleezy "you're in for it now look" as I knocked on his door.

"Come in," he growled.

I entered to see he and Russell standing there. Both looked pissed. Great.

I closed the door behind me and braced myself. Mac started by shouting, "Where in the hell have you been?"

"I took a personal day. I left Jessica a message--"

"And you decided to spend your day in Blount County for some reason?"

"How--"

"I got a call from Dr. Grace Allen at Blount County High

School. She was so sorry to hear we are investigating Regina Maynard and wanted to know if she could be of any further assistance."

"Oh."

"I told you specifically to stay out of this investigation!"

I nodded.

"And you ignored me! Do you want to lose your job? Because, I swear to God, Claire, I can and will let you go."

"I know."

Russell interjected. "Claire, I'm trying to get this investigation done, and I don't need you interfering!"

I nodded again.

"Please let me do my job."

"I'm sorry, but Grant is totally blindsided. He's worked so hard to get his company up and successful. He can't lose it. He just can't."

"I can't help him with you in the way," Russell said.

Mac said, "And I told you to stay out of it."

"I know."

"So stay out of it!"

"I will."

"I mean it!"

"I know." I was ready to get out of here. "I'm going to go back to work."

Mac nodded picked up an unlit cigar from his desk and looked at it longingly. "Both of you, get out." He gestured toward the door with the cigar.

I left quickly, Russell behind me. We made our way back to our office. He didn't say anything to me after we sat down.

"Russ?"

"Not now. I am really pissed at you."

"But don't you want to know what I learned?"

Silence.

"Dr. Allen thinks that Dylan's father is a guy named Jerry Cook. Have you pulled his birth certificate yet?"

He wrote the name down on a sticky note on his desk. "I haven't had a chance yet."

"Do you want me to do it? I can go talk to Michele."

"You might as well. You are going to anyway."

I went to the fourth floor. I was tired of justifying my actions. I knew I shouldn't be doing what I was doing, but I wanted Grant cleared.

Michele was a friend of mine, as well as one of our record keepers, along with Dolly, who managed the physical files in the record room in the basement. The agency had been talking about going all-digital for years, but so far had not made much progress. Michele's office was upstairs in what was once the customer service department when this building was Barwick's Department Store many years ago. Her office was surrounded by glass and had a sliding window. I knocked on it.

She slid the window open. "What's up?"

"I'm here for Russell. Looking for a birth cert on a kid named Dylan Maynard. Mom is Regina Maynard."

She typed what I said on her keyboard on her desk. In a moment, her printer spit out a sheet of paper which she handed to me.

"Thanks," I said.

"Hey, you okay?"

I gave her a small smile. "I'm having a rough day. I'll be okay."

"Is that the lady who's accused Grant?"

Wow, word gets around fast, I thought. "Yeah, this is her."

"I'm sorry about that. He'll get cleared."

"I hope so. How are the kids?"

A broad smile crossed her face. "Ian has decided on Auburn for college, and Kate is babysitting."

I returned the smile. Michele's kids were two of my very favorite young people, and it was good to hear they were doing well. She closed the window as I read the birth certificate. Dylan Gerald Maynard was born six years ago on January 12 at St. Vincent's Hospital of Blount County. No father was noted on the form. I wondered if Jerry had filed anything to be recognized in court. Or if Jerry's full name was Gerald. I headed back to my office and handed the form to Russell. "No father named."

"Not surprised."

"Me neither. What's next?"

"Claire—"

"I know, I know."

"I know you have work to do."

I sat at my desk and thought about that. I had two cases to close, and Mac had been nagging me about that for a week or so via email. I fetched the files from the filing cabinet in our office and started the paperwork.

After a few minutes, Russell said, "By the way, I'm interviewing Regina and Dylan at one tomorrow. They are coming here and I've booked the assessment room. If you want to watch, I figure I could use a second set of eyes."

Chapter Five

"You sure?"

"Just don't tell Mac. You've met this kid, so I want your opinion."

"Yeah, but I've only met him for like a minute."

"I think anything would help."

"Thanks. Really."

"It better not come back to bite me."

I got both my cases closed and took the files to Mac's office, dropping them off with Jessica and filling out a form rescinding my hours off for today. Jessica handed me a new case that had been reported by a daycare alleging neglect. It didn't appear at first to be anything too urgent, and I spent the rest of the afternoon on the phone making appointments to talk to the teachers and the parents. I kept my schedule free for Thursday at one.

Thursday morning, I went to the daycare that alleged the neglect against the two sisters, then to their home. It wasn't really neglect, honestly, the girls were just dirty because the family's water had been cut off due to lack of payment. I went back to the office and made some referrals and put the case in my "to be closed" file. At one o'clock, I made my way to the assessment room.

The assessment room was on the first floor on the east side of the building. It was a large room that had been painted in a happy, pastel yellow. Toys were scattered throughout the space, including a large, non-gender-specific dollhouse and several anatomically correct dolls. A table flanked by two chairs held paper and colored pencils. There was a bookshelf of books about families, too. Two denim bean-bag chairs were in there as well, on the colorful floor mat in the form of a jigsaw puzzle. I sat in the observation room so I could watch through the one-way mirror. I made sure the camera next to me was recording and dimmed the lights.

After a few minutes, Russ entered with little Dylan, who looked exactly as he had when I saw him last. Maybe a little taller. Skinny kid, dressed in clean, gray cargo shorts and a royal blue t-shirt with a gray truck on it. His clothes were a little big on him, but he would grow into them soon. His hair was dark brown and shaggy, like he hadn't had a haircut in a while. He had big, curious, blue eyes. His fair skin was slightly pink from a mild sunburn.

He went immediately to the table with the paper and colored pencils on it, that was just below the observation window. He started to pick up a pencil and stopped, looking at Russell. "Can I color?" He asked in a small voice.

"Sure, we can color if you want to." Russell sat in the other chair at the table. He asked permission before coloring, I thought, so impulse control was pretty good so far. Over the years, I had seen so many kids bolt into that room and tear through all the toys before I could even catch up.

Dylan chose a green pencil and drew some grass on a piece of paper. Then he chose black and drew a road. A small truck was next, colored red, with a brown-haired figure behind the steering wheel. Russell asked if he knew why he was here. He shrugged. "I'm supposed to talk about Mr. Grant."

"What about Mr. Grant?"

"I'm supposed to say he touched me."

"What can you tell me about that?"

"He touched me."

"Can you tell me more about it?"

"He touched me."

"Can you tell me where?"

"In the bathroom."

I saw Russell choke back a giggle. "I'm sorry, I wasn't clear. I meant where on your body."

Dylan started squirming, drawing huge roll bars on the truck. He shook his head.

"Dylan, remember we talked about this before we came in here. This is very serious. I need you to tell me the truth. You won't get in trouble for saying the truth, ever. Can you point to where he touched you?"

Dylan waved a hand toward his lap. "Down there. I don't want to talk about this anymore."

"Okay, I appreciate your being honest with me. Your truck looks great! Does your mommy drive a truck?"

"No, we have a Kia but it's little and doesn't work most

of the time. Mommy says she is going to get us a truck, as soon as she gets some money."

"How does mommy get money? Does she have a job?"

"She used to work for Mr. Grant, but she doesn't anymore. It's sad. He was nice."

"I thought you said he touched you."

I could see the moment of panic on little Dylan's face. He was caught in the deception and he knew it. He shrugged. "I don't know."

Russ focused on the truck again. After a moment, he asked, "Where would you go in that truck, if you could drive it?"

"I don't know." Dylan drew headlights on the truck, coloring them yellow. He was shutting down.

"Is there anything else you want to talk about, before I go get your mom?"

"I don't know."

"Last chance."

"No." It was practically a whisper.

"Okay, I'm going to go get your mom." Russ left to get Regina while I continued to watch Dylan. After Russ left, he continued coloring on the picture. He drew a large mountain behind the truck, outlined in brown. Several large objects were drawn on the top of the pointed mountain that looked like boulders. Then a gray thundercloud.

Russ and Regina walked in the room and, without being asked, Dylan took his picture and went and sat on one of the bean bag chairs so the adults could sit on the chairs by the table. Regina was artificially orange-tan, with long dark brown hair and blue eyes like her son's. Her body was larger than I remembered; she had gained some weight. She wore a lot of eye makeup that was a bright blue color, and her fire engine red lipstick wasn't doing her any favors. Her expression made me think she was annoyed.

Dylan was anxious. He was hyper-focused on his mom, and seemed to be waiting for her to say something. Acknowledge him, or anything. Russell asked how things were going.

"How do you think things are going for God's sake? My

son has been abused. What did he tell you? Did he tell you the details?"

Dylan shrank small in the bean bag as Russell answered, "I'm sorry, but everything Dylan and I discuss is between us, like I said before we started. Is he having any behavioral problems?"

"No. Should he be?"

Russell shrugged. "I'm just getting an idea of what's going on."

"When will Grant be arrested? When will the charges be filed?"

"I am going to refer Dylan to the Cole Center for further evaluation. They'll do an assessment and determine whether to send the case to the District Attorney for review."

"So all this was for nothing?" She shouted. "What the hell is the point of us coming down here then?" She stood up, as did Russ.

Dylan tucked his knees up to his chest on the bean bag. The poor kid was practically in the fetal position.

Russell continued, "This is the first step in any investigation. We'll refer it out from here and see what they are able to determine."

"Oh, for fuck's sake." Regina grabbed her purse and loudly said, "C'mon Dylan. Let's get out of here."

Dylan stood up and Russell addressed him. "It was great to meet you, Dylan. Thanks for talking to me. Can I keep your picture?"

He nodded and handed it to Russell as Regina stormed out of the room. Dylan followed her and I heard Russell sigh as I turned off the camera. He walked them out toward the lobby, then joined me the observation room after I turned up the lights.

Chapter Six

"Wow." I said to Russell.

"Right? What a dynamic." He handed me the picture and asked, "What do you think?"

None of what we thought about the drawing was going to be admissible in court, I knew. It was too subjective. I studied the piece of paper. "Impulse control was impressive for a six-year-old. Everything on here is small in scale, which could indicate anxiety. He started by drawing the road and the truck, possibly showing a desire to leave his current situation. Maybe the one here or the one at home. He is driving the truck, so he is taking control in the picture. No extreme phallic symbols or anything immediately indicating sexual abuse. Or psychosis for that matter. When you starting talking about his mother, he drew protective elements on the truck—roll bars and headlights. When you left to go get her, he drew the threats to the truck—the boulders and the clouds. In short, I'd say he is afraid of her."

"Hell, I'm afraid of her."

I laughed. "Right? Poor kid. I didn't think he could get any smaller on that bean bag. Did she say where she was living?"

"With her parents in Blount County. She's also convinced Dylan has Attention Deficit Disorder. She's looking for a psychiatrist to certify that fact so she can apply for disability."

I rolled my eyes and handed the drawing back to Russell. "Christ. He's the least ADD or ADHD kid I've ever seen. And she admitted he is not having any behavioral problems, so that's never going to fly."

Russell stretched his shoulders and said, "I'm going to make a referral to the Cole Center just to cover our asses, but I don't think anything is going to come of it."

"I don't either. I'm more worried that she's dragging him from doctor to doctor trying to convince everyone he is sick."

"You thinking Munchausen's by Proxy? What's it called, now?"

"Factitious Disorder. Maybe not that extreme, but it's got to be stressful for little Dylan."

"True."

"Thanks for letting me observe."

"Thanks for not busting in there and beating her up."

"Tempted."

"I know."

I picked Reese up at four-thirty at Dad's. They had gotten several boxes filled with giveaway items and taken them down the hill to Goodwill. I reminded Reese that we needed to go grocery shopping.

"Oh, yeah." She looked at Dad. "Grant's coming over for dinner tomorrow. I'm making dinner."

"Really?" Dad asked me.

"Yeah, I talked to him earlier in the week and asked him over."

"I hope it goes well. I was sorry to see him go."

"Me, too."

Reese and I hit the Piggly Wiggly in our neighborhood. The store was relatively new and the produce there was spectacular. I gathered baby spinach, parmesan, and croutons to make a salad with garlic vinaigrette while Reese went to get chicken and angel hair pasta and mushrooms. I got a six-pack of Grant's favorite beer, Fat Tire, and bought myself a bottle of the Sauvignon Blanc I liked. I let LaReesa pick the bottle of Marsala wine and I asked her if there was anything else she needed.

She looked around to make sure no one was listening. "I need stuff for my monthlies."

"Okay." We found the isle with feminine products and she chose what she needed. Back in January, I had started her on birth control just to be extra safe. When she ran away last year, she stayed with a young man named Roderick who had pimped her out for money. I had offered to help her press charges, but she had declined. Luckily her tests for STDs were all negative and she had avoided a pregnancy by some miracle. She said she wasn't sleeping with anyone, and wasn't planning to, but I felt safer knowing she had some pregnancy protection, anyway. It also helped her hormones be more manageable.

We got home and unloaded all the stuff. Reese's phone chimed several times while we were unloading, and when we finished, she checked it. "Sharonda wants to do something on Saturday. Can I?"

"What does she want to do?"

"Can she come over here? She wants to go for a walk."

"Well, that sounds very healthy."

She rolled her eyes at me. "She has a crush on some guy named Elijah who lives in those townhouses down by the grocery store. She wants to walk by his house and hope he comes outside."

I laughed. I had done the exact same thing when I was thirteen and fourteen, strolling casually by a house where a boy named William lived, only to be struck dumb and mute when he finally walked outside. Reese continued, "It's so stupid. I tol' her, if you like him, jus' talk to him."

"For some girls, that's absolutely terrifying." The townhouses she referred to were close to the Pig we had just left, not but a mile away. "Anyway, it'll be good exercise."

"Ugh. I'll tell her to come over around one, okay?"

"That sounds fine. Do you have a crush on anybody?"

"Naw. All them boys in school are so lame. They just act a fool all the time."

"They are immature."

"Totally."

"In some men, that never changes."

"You got you a good one, though, right? I mean, Grant never did nothin' stupid."

"No, that was me. He had his faults, though."

"Like what?"

"He was difficult to communicate with sometimes. If he was mad or overwhelmed, he would shut me out."

"Do you think he got mad when you let me live here?"

"No! No, hon, please don't ever think that. He was fine with it." Funny, I had just stated Grant was hard to communicate with, but I was the one who had brought a teenager home in the middle of the night without even discussing it with him. Maybe I was the one with the problem.

Chapter Seven

Friday was a day of total chaos. One of my teenage clients objected to his placement in a foster home and threatened to run away. Then he threatened to kill himself and cut his wrists a bit with a steak knife. The suicide attempt was half-assed, but I spent all day trying to get him a bed in a local psychiatric hospital just in case. I finally accomplished that task before leaving at four-twenty to pick up Reese. When I got to Dad's at ten to five, she was ticked at me.

"Where the hell you been?"

"I'm sorry. I've had a long day."

"Ain't all your days long days?"

"Yeah, now that you mention it."

"What time is Grant comin' over?

"He'll be at the house at five, he said."

We got home and I had time to change into shorts and a clean top before the doorbell rang. He was right on time, which was encouraging. He came to the front door, which he never used to do. That stung a bit, knowing he felt like a visitor. *And that's your fault,* I told myself as I answered the door. He had khaki shorts on and a crimson Alabama football t-shirt.

"Hey, come on in. Love that shirt. Roll Tide!"

I got a smile for that comment. He handed me a bouquet of beautiful flowers, filled with my favorite pink carnations and white daisies. "Thank you! These are gorgeous. LaReesa's in the kitchen."

He followed me through the living room and dining area, around to the galley style kitchen beyond. LaReesa was in there, mixing the flour, salt, pepper, and oregano for the chicken. She looked up when Grant entered, and suddenly the mood was a bit tense.

"Hi," she said.

"Hi. How are you?"

"Good. I passed math."

"I heard. I'm proud of you. You worked hard."

Reese smiled at that and took a small step toward him. He opened his arms and she rushed into them and gave him a big hug around his waist, which he returned. I turned away, suddenly a little choked up.

"I'm making you chicken marsala. You still like Italian food, right?"

"Love it."

"I'm going to go get a vase," I said, and walked out the nearby door to the storage room at the back of the carport where the shelves above the washing machine and dryer held all sorts of general stuff: Camping equipment, kitchen ware, vases, and some pottery I didn't have any space for in the house. I chose a tall, light green, dimpled vase that featured a painted daisy on the side and took a moment to collect myself. I was shaking.

I inhaled a few deep breaths and went back into the house. Grant and Reese were still in the kitchen, talking, and I could overhear them.

LaReesa said, "...doin' okay, but she ain't datin' nobody. She works all the damn time. She misses you. I miss you."

"I miss you guys, too."

I walked the door of the kitchen and asked Grant, "You want a beer?"

"Sure."

I put the flowers in the vase with cold water and put them on a trivet on the dining room table just outside the kitchen, then grabbed a Fat Tire from the fridge and handed it to him. I opened the bottle of Sauv Blanc and poured myself a glass. "Wanna sit outside?"

"Sounds great."

We went out to the deck behind the house. The deck had been untouched since I bought the place over a year ago and was looking a bit run down. It needed to be re-stained, something I had been meaning to do but hadn't found the time yet. I sat in one of the four black wrought-iron chairs and Grant sat next to me. The temperature outside was minimally cooler since the sun was going to set in a couple of hours. The birds fed at the hanging feeder in the yard. We used to sit outside together when he lived here and I remembered those times with fondness.

"I see you still haven't re-stained the deck."

"Haven't found the time. Maybe I'll get it done this summer."

He laughed. "Somehow I doubt that."

I smiled at him. "Yeah, me too. I saw Regina and Dylan yesterday, but don't tell anyone I told you that. They came down to DHS for a meeting with Russell."

"How did it go?" He sipped the beer.

"I don't think you have anything to worry about. Little Dylan wasn't really forthcoming with a lot of details."

"Because it's not true."

"I know. Russ is going to refer them to an agency that specializes in getting testimony from children for these types of cases, but I don't think anything will come of it."

"God damn her. The D.A. is lumping all the charges of theft against her together and is hoping to get a longer sentence. Convict her of Second-degree or First-degree Theft instead of just a misdemeanor."

"How do they determine that?"

"It depends on the value of what was stolen."

"Does your attorney know she's been accused before, in Blount County?"

"What?"

"I went up there on Wednesday just to ask around. She worked at a restaurant called Grandma's Apron. She stole credit card numbers, but the owner said they didn't press charges. They were trying to be kind since she was a teenager, and had a new baby."

Grant pulled out his phone and began to type on it. "I'm sending myself a reminder to let the attorneys know that on Monday. Thanks for looking into that for me."

I took a deep breath. "I'd do anything to help you." My voice was breaking a bit. "Anything."

The look on his face was tender as his green eyes met mine. I felt my eyes begin to fill with tears and looked away, quickly sipping the wine and trying to get myself under control.

"I don't know how I could have been so stupid, hiring her."

"You're a sweet, big-hearted guy, and you wanted to

help."

"Well, it sure bit me in the ass."

Reese came out of the door, drying her hands on a dish towel. "Dinner about six-thirty? Is that okay?"

"Perfect." I said.

Grant gestured toward one of the metal chairs across from us. "Come talk to me. Tell me how you've been."

She sat. "I'm good. I'm helpin' Papa Doc get rid of some stuff in his house."

"Is he going to sell it?" Grant asked.

"He's thinking about it," Reese answered. "Says he ain't got no use for a three-bedroom house no more."

"He hasn't said anything to me about that." I said, suddenly concerned. I hated to think of my childhood home, sold to someone else.

"He ain't made no decision yet, so don't worry." LaReesa said. "He said he done lived there a long time and can't imagine nowhere else."

I nodded. The house was a lot to handle, and I wasn't surprised he was thinking about something smaller.

LaReesa focused on Grant. "How's things with you? I mean, I heard about what that bitch said about you. I wanna fu--, I mean, I wanna mess her up."

"Thank you for watching your language." I looked at Grant. "We are working on that."

Grant smiled at Reese. "Yes, thank you. Work is going well. I'm staying busy despite everything. I've hired two new I.T. people, and we are bidding to outfit the new hospital west of here. I'm hoping that comes through. That, and just basic computer repairs are keeping us busy."

"I'm glad it's going well." I said.

"Where you livin' now?" Reese asked.

"I bought a house."

"Cool!" Reese said.

"Did you?" I asked at the same time.

Grant smiled. "I did. It was time to make that investment, instead of paying rent. It's down the hill, off South Shades Crest Road. In a neighborhood called Russet Woods. It's three bedrooms and a full basement. I love it, although right now

40

it's filled with stuff I need to unpack."

"Well, congratulations!" I said.

"Thanks. I'd love to show it to you both sometime."

I glanced at LaReesa with a smile. "We'd love that."

Reese stood up. "I have to go finish dinner." She picked up the dishtowel and went inside.

"Russet Woods is a huge neighborhood," I said. "Aren't there like a thousand houses in there?"

"A little over that, yeah. But it's a nice one, safe, and diverse. I like it. The schools are good, and whatever happens I won't lose money."

"Be a good place to raise a family."

"It will. Someday." Something in his voice was soft, and…longing. I felt a lump rise in my throat and sipped my last sip of wine. "Do you want another beer?"

"I'd love one." I went into the kitchen and grabbed another Fat Tire and another glass of wine. LaReesa had grated the cheese and was tossing the salad. I checked the time and it was six p.m. I brought the beer out to Grant, who stood at the edge of the deck kicking at a piece of wood. "This really needs to be re-stained before it rots."

"Okay. Maybe I can hire someone to do that next week."

"I can do it. Tomorrow, if you like."

"You don't have to do that. Don't you have your own house to worry about?"

"Mine was turn-key ready. New floors and all. There's not much to do, but I do have to buy some furniture. Really, I'll come over tomorrow with my pressure washer and get it done, if you'll go get some stain and some rollers."

"I appreciate it. You sure don't owe me anything, after what I did." I looked at the deck, shame filling my face and turning it red.

"Maybe we are both to blame for what happened."

"No, it was all me. It was impulsive, and stupid. It was done in a time of stress and I knew better. I will regret it for the rest of my life and I am really, really sorry."

"I accept your apology. I hope we can be friends."

That started the damn tears again. I wiped my eyes and said, "Dammit."

Grant laughed. "I don't think I've ever seen you cry."

"Hell, it happens all the time now. I'm a damn Weepy Wendy."

He laughed again and said, "It's a little nice to know you miss me."

"A lot."

Chapter Eight

I wiped my eyes again and sipped even more wine. I needed to eat at the rate I was drinking. "I think I'm going to go check on dinner."

I went into the house where Reese was finishing the salad with the croutons. The kitchen smelled heavenly and Reese said the only thing she had to do was put the bread in the oven for a few minutes. She whispered in my ear, "How is it going?"

"Good, I think. He doesn't hate me, so that's something. He's going to come over tomorrow and work on the deck."

"That's sweet."

"He's a sweet guy."

Dinner was delicious and both Grant and I praised Reese's cooking skills throughout the meal. Reese beamed at that and even offered to do the dishes afterwards. I walked Grant out.

He leaned his long body against the door of his minivan. "Thanks for dinner. LaReesa's a good cook."

"Yeah, I'm happy she is developing some interest and skill that may get her an honest job someday. She still says she wants to do hair, though."

"Well, she's got years to make all those decisions."

"If she stays on a straight path. There are days when it's a struggle."

"I think you are doing well with her, though."

"I hope so."

"I'll see you tomorrow. What time?"

"I have to go to the store and get the stain, but I can be home by eleven?"

"Sounds good."

Things between us were suddenly a little awkward. The last time we'd parted here was when he stormed off after handing me his key with his van full of his things. I fidgeted, not knowing what to do. It was weird to part without a hug, or a kiss. "Well, bye," I ventured.

"Can I have a hug?"

"Of course."

He bent over and slid his arms around my waist. My arms went up around his neck and the whole action was just so comfortable and natural. It felt like home. He held me longer than I expected and said "See you tomorrow," with a smile as he entered the van and cranked it. I felt a glimmer of hope as I watched him drive down the street.

I was at Lowe's by ten Saturday morning, and it didn't take long to get a gallon of solid tan stain and some rollers, along with a pole to extend the handle of the roller so he could stand up while staining. I got home about ten-thirty and had to rouse Reese out of bed. She groaned when I told her it was time to get up.

"It's ten-thirty, Lazy Lady. Up. Grant will be here in half an hour and I think you might want to be dressed, no?"

"I'm goin', Jeez." She headed for the bathroom with an armful of clothes.

Grant arrived about the time Reese got out of the bathroom. He had his pressure washer and hooked it up to the hose outside while we chatted.

"This is going to be a little loud. Sorry," he said.

"It's okay. I appreciate your doing this on a Saturday when you could be doing other things."

"I'm happy to help." He squeezed the wand of the pressure washer, and pulled the starter cord. It roared to life and he began to guide it around the deck. I stood and watched for a few minutes, watching the old, gray deck turn more golden and enjoying the illusion of domesticity.

I went back in the house and thought about what to do next. Reese was in her room with the door shut. I had multiple loads of laundry to do and thought that would be a good place to start. I sorted three loads and started one.

Two hours later, Grant came in the house and stated he was finished with the pressure washing. "It has to dry overnight before I can stain it," he said. "Can I come back tomorrow?"

"Of course," I said. "You sure I can't pay you for this, or something?"

"No, of course not."

The front doorbell rang and I went and opened the door. LaReesa's best friend, Sharonda Fowler, stood there and greeted me with, "Hey, Miss Conover." Sharonda was a thin black girl, always cutely dressed, but today she looked especially nice in shorts and a pink-patterned top. Her black hair was done in long braids, just like LaReesa's.

Her mother was watching from the SUV in the driveway. I waved to her, calling "Hey, Cheryl!"

"Hi! I'll pick her up about five, okay?"

"That's fine, or I can run her home."

"You sure you don't mind?"

"I can do it. It's fine."

She waved a final wave and backed out of the driveway. Sharonda entered the house and spotted Grant. "Oh, hi," she said.

"Hi, Sharonda."

"Reese's in her room," I said to her and she walked that way down the hall. We heard her knocking on the door and Reese opening it.

Grant's phone dinged and he pulled it out of his pocket. I watched as he read the text and his face turned to concern, then paled a bit.

"You okay? What's up?"

He handed me the phone. It was a text from Regina Maynard.

You are going to regret what you've done.
That bitch ex-girlfriend of yours can't help you.
She is not going to be able to stop Dylan from telling on you.
I will kill you.
And her.
And those two black girls too.
Just wait.

"Jesus," I said. "She's watching this house."

"She's following me. I've suspected for a while now that she might be. This just confirms it."

I pulled out my phone. "I'm calling the police." I dialed

45

911 and when the dispatcher answered I asked for an officer to my address and explained someone was threatening me. I hung up just as Reese and Sharonda walked in the room.

"Hey, we are going for a walk," Reese said.

"No!" Grant and I both said at the same time, forcefully.

"What? Why not? You said--"

"Just sit down, both of you." I pointed to the couch.

"But--"

"LaReesa, please. Sit down for a second and let us explain. The police are on the way here and we need to talk first." Grant was closing the plantation blinds on the front window.

That got her to sit, wide eyed. Sharonda sat next to her and Grant and I sat in the chairs facing them. I looked and Grant and nodded at him to tell the story.

"A few months ago, in January, I fired someone. A woman named Regina who worked at my shop."

"I remember her. She the one who done--"

Grant held up a hand to stop her talking. "She was stealing from me, and from my clients. I had her arrested and she is going to trial in August for theft. Now she is following me, and threatening me. She just sent a text that makes us think she is nearby. We have called the police and they are on their way. So, we want you to stay inside for a bit."

"What she done said? I'm going to fuck her up so bad."

"Language, LaReesa."

Grant looked at me. "Should I show them?"

"They might as well know, since they are involved."

He passed his cell phone to Reese who took it and read the text. "I'm gonna--"

"Let the police handle it." I finished.

"She done accused you of messin' with her kid, right? That ain't true. She a liar."

"And a thief," I said. "The police and the system have a way of dealing with her, and we are going to let them do their jobs and handle this."

LaReesa scoffed. "I guess the system works for white people." Sharonda nodded beside her.

"The system works for everyone, if you let it," I said. "I

46

need you to stay inside for a while. Do you remember what she looks like?"

Reese nodded, and looked at Sharonda. "White lady with long brown hair, a bad tan and a big ass—oops, hips."

I added, "I need you to tell an adult and call 911 if you see her, okay? Promise me."

"I promise but damn."

A police SUV pulled up to the curb and I asked the girls to go to Reese's room so we could talk to the officer. Grant took the lead and explained everything to the cop who agreed to file a report and have the patrol officers drive by a few times a day. Grant took a screen shot of the text and printed it on my printer for the police, then forwarded the text to me.

I told the officer that I knew she drove a Kia but I didn't know what type or what color. Grant said it was a Kia Rio and it was white. The officer wrote everything down and said Grant could pick up a copy of the report late next week if he wanted to. We thanked him for coming out and after he left, I asked Grant what was next.

"I think I'm going to have an alarm installed at my new house. Do you still have the one I got you?"

Grant had given me an alarm last year, when I had been threatened while investigating little Michael Hennessy's death. "That thing? It ran on my land line, which has been gone for months. I don't even know where it is."

"Will you let me install something here? I'd feel better if you did."

"You really think she's going to come after me?"

'I don't know what she is going to do, and I'd feel better knowing you are safe. This is, after all, my fault."

"You couldn't have predicted what she was going to do. Do you have a gun?"

"That's my next stop."

"Really?"

"Really. I'm heading to Mark's Outdoors before they close."

"You don't think that's overkill? No pun intended."

"I don't know what she is capable of. And she's threatened me and people I care about."

The tears welled again and I looked away and collected myself.

"What?" he asked.

"It's nice to hear you say you care about me. And LaReesa."

"Of course, I do. I always will. I'll be back tomorrow to stain the deck. What time do you think?"

"Anytime."

"I'll be here about eleven again, then."

I got another hug before he left, and another smile, which made my day. I went back to Reese's room after he was gone and knocked on the door.

"Come in," Reese said.

She and Sharonda sat on the floor, talking. I joined them, leaning my back against Reese's bed and crossing my legs in front of me. "I wanted to see if you two had any concerns, or questions."

Reese said, "You think she out there, watching us?"

"I think it's possible, based on the text. If she had just mentioned one black girl, I might not be so worried, because she knows you live with me. But she mentioned two. And that has me concerned. I think the best thing to do now is to have Sharonda go home."

"Can Reese come spend the night with me? I texted my mom what happened." Sharonda asked.

I thought about that. It would be great to have her out of the house and someplace safer, but I didn't want to drag Sharonda's parents into this. I voiced this to the girls as Sharonda's phone dinged. She read the text.

"Mamma says to go ahead and bring her over for a couple of days. She's happy to help."

"Please, Claire?" Reese added.

"Okay, pack some clothes."

"What about you?"

"I think I will go stay at Dad's tonight, if he's okay with that."

LaReesa packed some things in a duffel bag and gathered her bathroom items and I did the same. The drive to the Fowlers was less than ten minutes. I walked the girls to the

48

door of the Fowler's house and waited while Sharonda went to find her mom. Cheryl joined me just inside the front door after welcoming us both. The girls headed up the beautiful staircase in front of us.

"You okay?" Cheryl asked me.

"Yeah, I'm fine. Sharonda told you what happened?"

"She said a woman is threatening you and Grant. I didn't know you two were back together."

"Oh we aren't. At least not yet, and maybe not ever. I probably screwed that up permanently. He fired this woman in January and now she's making all kinds of threats. I wouldn't be worried but she specifically mentioned two girls in her latest threat, so I'm grateful Reese can be somewhere safe."

"We are happy to help. I can send her home whenever you like."

"I'm hoping to have some sort of security installed next week. Then I'll feel better about us staying there."

"Just let me know. We'll take Reese to church tomorrow if that's okay."

"I think that's great if she'll go."

"I asked her about it once and she seemed very interested."

"Really?"

Cheryl winked at me. "It's a Black thing."

I laughed. "Thank you."

I left Cheryl's and headed down Shades Crest Road to Dad's house. I pulled into his driveway and checked the time on my dashboard. It was ten after four. I gathered my overnight bag and walked to the front door. It was locked, but Dad's Prius was in the drive. No matter, I thought, I had a key. I fished it out of my purse and entered the house.

"Dad?" I called. "Dad?"

He wasn't in the kitchen. "Dad?"

I entered the living room, and saw him sitting on the couch.

With a woman. She had her legs thrown over his lap and their arms were around each other.

I stood there, in shock, as Dad and the woman separated and they both stood up. Dad said, "Claire! What are you doing here?"

"I'm sorry. I should have called. I'll go." I turned back toward the kitchen.

"No, no, you don't have to. What's with the luggage?"

"It's a long story. Who's your friend?" I asked, nodding toward the thin gray-haired lady who was straightening her light blue button-down blouse.

"This is Vicky."

"Hi," she said to me.

"I'm so sorry to interrupt. Really, I can go."

Dad said, "What's going on? Come sit down." He gestured to one of the chairs in the room. I sat.

"I told you about Grant and Regina." I looked at Vicky. "Grant is my ex-boyfriend, and in January he fired this woman, Regina, who is now threatening him. And me. And my foster daughter." I pulled out my phone and showed them the text that Grant had forwarded to me earlier.

Dad's brow creased with concern. "Where is Reese?" he asked.

"She's staying down the street with the Fowlers for a couple of days. I was hoping I could sleep in my old room tonight and maybe tomorrow? I'd feel safer, but I don't want to mess up your plans."

"Of course you can. Did you call the police?"

"We did. An officer came out and took a report. Grant is going to confer with his lawyers on Monday. You sure you don't mind if I stay?"

"Not at all. Vicky and I were going to go out to dinner, but we can just as easily order in."

"You two can go. I can stay here."

Vicky said, "Actually, I think I will head home. Claire, it was nice to meet you. I've heard a lot about you from Christopher."

"I'm so sorry."

"It's fine. There will be other nights to go out."

"I have to run her home," Dad said. "I won't be too long."

They left, and I went back to my old room to put my bag down. I surveyed the familiar sight with a sense of comfort. My pink and green floral comforter covered the old twin bed, same as always, and matched the light pink paint on the walls. I put my bag on the bed and went to inspect what was in the kitchen.

My father was a part-time vegetarian. I'll say this, he tried hard. But often when we ate together and I ordered a meat dish, half of it would be eaten by him. His fridge revealed nothing but a half-gone head of iceberg lettuce, a soggy tomato, and some yogurt.

I went to the den and flopped down in the recliner, reaching for the remote to turn on the TV. The local news was on, which I watched with semi-focused interest until I heard Dad's Prius turn into the driveway. He entered the house a few moments later.

"You okay?" he asked.

"Yeah, I'm fine. Thanks for letting me stay tonight. Vicky seems very nice. How did you two meet?"

"She's in my water aerobics class at the Rec. She's widowed, too. Her husband died of pancreatic cancer six years ago, so we have that in common."

'What a thing to build a relationship on."

"I know, right? She's very nice, has a house over on Deo Dara Drive, by the country club."

"Nice. How long have you been seeing her?"

"About four months."

"Four months! Were you ever going to mention her to me?"

"I was getting around to it. How did it go with Grant?"

"Fine, until that text. He pressure-washed my deck for me, and will stain it tomorrow."

"Nice of him."

"I know. He sure doesn't owe me anything."

"He's that kind of guy."

"I know that. Now. Maybe I always did, but I didn't appreciate it."

We decided on pizza for dinner, and ordered a veggie one and had it delivered. I went to bed shortly after dinner, crawling into my old bed with a sense of comfort and warmth. I lay there and listened to all the old familiar sounds for a while: the occasional car driving by outside, the hum of the air conditioner as it turned on and off, and the sounds of my father rustling around in his room across the hall. I texted Reese, and she said she and Sharonda were watching a movie in her room and were in for the night.

I woke the next morning after restless sleep and met my father in the kitchen, where he was pouring water into the back of the coffee maker. I stayed for a cup, then showered and was home by ten-thirty.

I pulled into the carport on the left side of the house. The door to the house was up three brick stairs. I pulled my key out of my purse and opened the door. The key felt different in the lock, and I wondered if I had remembered to lock it when I left. I couldn't remember.

The door entered to the dining area, where Grant's flowers still graced the table.

But something was wrong. Something was different.

The flowers had been moved.

Chapter Nine

Pink carnations are my favorite flower, and I had been delighted yesterday to receive six of them, plus a dozen daisies. I had placed them in that tall vase that was a textured green and white with a painted flower on one side. I faced the flower design toward the kitchen, but now it faced the wall. And one of the carnations was missing.

All my nerves tingled a bit, but I shoved down the fear and anger as I looked around the rest of the house, phone in hand ready to dial 911. Nothing was disturbed in the living room that I could see. Nothing appeared to be missing. I inspected LaReesa's room and couldn't see anything bothered there. Not that I could really tell, since it was such a mess. My office was next, and my laptop still sat on the antique roll-top desk against the wall. I went in my bedroom, where my blue-and-white bed was made neatly, pillows and throw pillows in place.

A pink carnation stem, along with the bloom that had been ripped off it, sat on one of my pillows.

I called Grant.

"Hey, I'm on my way," he answered. "I just left my house. I'm sorry I'm running a little late."

"Somebody broke in here. I'm calling the cops."

"What? Wait, I'll be there in ten." He hung up.

I locked all the doors and sat in the living room and waited. My house, my little sanctuary that I loved so much, had been violated. Invaded. Mad didn't even cover what I felt. I was furious. Scared, and hurt. I opened the blinds and watched for Grant from the window.

His van roared up to the curb and he exited, slamming the door behind him. I studied the neighborhood around him, wondering if Regina had followed him like he suspected. I didn't see any cars. I unlocked the front door as he walked up to the front door, then let him in.

"Are you okay?" he asked.

"Not really. I'm shook up." I answered. "Come see."

I showed him the vase of flowers, which I had not touched. "I put the design on the vase facing toward the kitchen," I pointed to the vase as I spoke. "Now it's toward the wall, and there was a flower missing." I walked him back to the bedroom we had shared until January and showed him the destroyed carnation on the bed. Then we called the police.

The Hoover police responded quickly; I'll say that for them. It was a different officer from yesterday, so Grant had to go through the whole story again about Regina and the threats. The officer checked around the house but couldn't see any obvious point of entry. I asked about fingerprints. He studied the vase and said though they could maybe get partials, it wouldn't be likely because of the texture of the vase. And they'd have to match someone in the system. He noted that we were lucky, and nothing of real value had been stolen, nodding toward the TV. He said he'd file a report and we could pick it up in a week or so. I got the impression that he thought we were being a bit hysterical over one pulled-apart flower.

After he left, I collapsed on the sofa. "I feel like he didn't understand. We've been threatened, right?"

"We have. It's scary, but to him, it's just one damaged flower, so what's the big deal?"

"I feel so…"

"So what?"

"Violated. Really. I know that sounds ridiculous."

"Not at all. Someone has been in your space, uninvited, and you are not the only one who is freaked out."

He joined me on the couch and placed one of his long, strong arms around me, pulling me close to him until my head rested on his chest. I took a deep breath, inhaling the familiar scent that was uniquely his body and feeling myself relax into him.

"I'm so sorry," he said.

It was worth it, I thought. *Worth it to have you here with me like this.* "It's not your fault. She's nuts."

He laughed. "Seems so. I should go stain your deck."

"Yeah."

He didn't move, and neither did I.

After a few more minutes, I slowly sat up out of the warmth of his arms and stood up. "I guess this isn't getting any work done."

"Can I use your computer?"

"What for?"

"I'm going to order you some cameras. Have them shipped here and I'll install them next week. Hopefully tomorrow."

"Thank you."

I walked with him down the hall to my office. I woke up my laptop and logged in, and stood up so he could sit. After a few minutes of typing, he stood up and said, "There. You have three cameras arriving tomorrow. Can I come over after work and hook them up?"

"Of course."

"If she shows up again, we'll have some proof. I'm off to stain."

I watched from the window as he poured the tan stain into the paint pan and began to roll it on. The deck looked so much better already. Within an hour, he was finished. "Don't walk out there until tomorrow, okay?"

"Okay. Thanks so much, again."

"I'll be here tomorrow about four to do the cameras. Will you be here?"

"I'll try my best. You know, it depends on the day. I've got court in the morning and not much scheduled after, so we'll see."

"I'll see you then."

I spent the rest of the evening writing the report for the case I had on the docket the next morning. The client was a baby, aged three months, whose mother had gone into residential drug treatment and she had no local family.

Monday morning, I said hello to George, the bailiff, and told him a blonde joke, which were his favorites. "What does the blonde say when the doctor tells her she's pregnant?"

"What?"

"Is it mine?"

That answer earned me a giggle. George would retire soon, and I was going to miss him. After a few minutes, he called my case. The baby showed up with her foster family but mom was a no-show. I was surprised by that, and vocalized this to Judge Clayton Myer. Mom's drug tests had all come back clean, so the failure to appear was surprising. I knew there were a lot of reasons why people didn't come to their court dates, and sometimes it was something as simple as not having a ride. Still, I wished she would have called me. I made a note in my calendar to check on her tomorrow.

Back at the office, I sent Mac an email and stated I was taking two hours of comp time this afternoon because I had an appointment. I had hours and hours of time owed me, so I wasn't worried about it. As I was finishing the email, Russell entered the office. He flopped down in his chair and muttered, "That total bitch."

"Who's a total bitch?"

"Sorry. Your buddy, Regina."

I turned around in my chair. "What's she done now?"

"She lied to me."

"What?"

"She told me last week she was living with her parents in Blount County. I went all the way up Hayden to talk to them, and she doesn't live there. Her parents, who are truly lovely by the way, haven't seen her months. Since Christmas, they say. She stayed long enough to get a few gifts for her and Dylan and left. They have no idea where she is or where she is living."

"Sounds typical, for her. I can tell you where I think she was on Saturday afternoon."

"Where?"

I relayed the story of the text to Grant, and the fact that we had called the cops. I showed him the text and told Russ that Grant thought she was following him.

"Well, that would certainly be easier to do if she lives here. Does he have a recent address for her?"

"I can see." I found my phone and texted him. He texted back that she used to live at The Falls and Woods apartments in Hoover, so Russ used his phone to look up the number and called them. The nice lady on the phone informed him that there was no Regina Maynard living there. He tried to call Regina directly, but got her voice mail.

"She's ducking my calls."

"Most people do."

"Nice! Thanks!"

"Our calls, I mean. From DHS. Not just you."

Russ went to update Mac and I left to do a couple of home visits. Both went well, and I was in my driveway by three-forty. There was a large box on my front stoop from Amazon. Grant pulled up at three forty-five and I greeted him at the door.

"The cameras are on the dining room table."

Grant opened the large cardboard box and removed three light blue boxes with REOLINK printed in white on them. I watched as he opened one. The cameras were white and cylindrical, with each camera about the size of a juice glass. He held one up for me to see.

"You'll be able to see who is outside from your phone."

"Will I get alerts when something activates it?"

"Once you download the app. This is going to take me a little while, I'm afraid."

"No problem. I'm grateful to have them."

I updated Dad, telling him Grant was at my house and installing cameras so I would be sleeping here tonight. He texted back that I could pick up my stuff anytime.

Installing the cameras involved running wires through the walls and attic, apparently. Grant chose to place one camera toward the front door, mounted on the eave and facing downward so it showed the front stoop and my dark green door and part of the walk up to it. Then the second went in the carport, mounted in the corner and showing the door to the dining area. Another went in the back yard, again on the soffit and facing the back door.

Grant finished installing them just as the sun dipped beyond the horizon, about eight o'clock. I made us some sandwiches and he borrowed my phone to download the app. He showed me how to use it as we ate. "See, you can scroll through and see what's going on, on any of them. I've put the app on my phone, too, just for backup."

I looked at the view of my front walk on my phone. "This is cool. How are they powered?"

"The wires from the cameras are running to an Ethernet

switch in your office. I ran the wires through the wall so it's nice and neat."

"Thank you. What happens if the power goes off?"

"This has a battery backup with it. It's the tower looking thing sitting next to your grandmother's desk. You'll have about an hour of video after the power goes out."

"Thank you so much for doing this."

"Hopefully it will give us a little warning if Regina shows up again. It won't call the police for you, though, so you'll have to do that if someone shows up on it."

"What's the noise? Is it like a siren? I want it to wake me up at night if needed."

"Here," he took my phone again and pressed the screen a few times. Suddenly, a shrill whine sounded, making me wince.

"Oh, wow, yeah, that'll wake me up."

"That's the idea."

"Thanks so much, again."

"Let's hope we never have to use it. Or my new gun." He reached into the front pocket of his shorts and pulled out the tiniest gun I'd ever seen.

"That's it?"

"That's it. It's small enough to carry every day and no one can see that I have it. If, and that's a big if, I have to use it, I'm going to be very close to whoever I'm going to kill."

He handed me the revolver and I held it in my right hand. For something so small, it had a lot of weight. "What kind of bullets does it shoot?"

"That's a .22 caliber. It will kill someone up close."

I handed the gun back to him. "I sincerely hope you never have to use it."

"Me, too."

I yawned. I was tired, and needed to sleep, but I didn't want to say goodbye to him. I picked up the paper plates from the sandwiches and threw them away. It was nine p.m., and I knew I needed to get to bed.

Grant stood in the doorway to the kitchen and asked, "Are you okay here by yourself tonight? I mean, I could stay if you want me to."

Surprised, I raised my brow at him. He continued, "Oh, you know, not in your bed. I could sleep on the couch or something, I mean, if you want."

"That's very sweet. I think I'll be okay. I lived here alone before I met you, and before I met LaReesa."

"Yeah, but nobody was threatening you then. You sure you'll be okay?"

I smiled. I loved that he was concerned about me. "I think so. Thanks for worrying, though. I've missed that."

"Would you, um, want to have dinner this week sometime?"

The butterflies in my stomach fluttered again. "Like a date?"

"Yeah. Yeah, a date."

I looked down at the floor. "You sure? I mean, after what I di-"

"So is that a no?"

"No! I mean no it's not a no. It's a very happy yes."

"Wednesday? I can pick you up at six-thirty?"

"Perfect. And thanks. Thank you for forgiving me."

He leaned down and gave me a gentle kiss on the cheek before saying goodbye. The tears started again, but this time they were happy tears.

A half hour later, I crawled into my big, cozy bed with a smile on my face. I couldn't wait until Wednesday. I fell asleep wondering where we'd go.

At two-seventeen in the morning, I woke up to my phone screaming.

Chapter Ten

I grabbed for the shrilling phone on my nightstand and turned on the lamp next to me. Pulled up the app while walking to my bedroom door and locking it. I clutched the phone, ready to call 911. I silenced the alarm and pulled up the camera feed. Checked the carport first. Nothing. Checked the back door. Nothing.

The front door. There he was. In front of the door. I squinted at the screen to see a masked face surveying the space around him. He stood up tall.

I watched as his ears twitched. His tail shook as he dropped to all fours and waddled out to the front yard.

A raccoon. A fucking raccoon. I unlocked the bedroom door and took a deep breath as my phone rang, startling me and making me jump, again. My heart was pounding.

Grant. I answered it. "Hey."

"You okay?"

"There was a raccoon by the front door. Did you see it?"

"By the time I pulled up the camera, he was gone."

"Good thing I don't have a gun, there would have been raccoon bits everywhere. Scared me to death."

He chuckled, his voice hoarse and sexy and half-awake. "That's the only downside to the motion sensors. They alert to everything."

"That's okay. I'd rather have false alarms than no alarms." I walked to the front door and began to turn on the lights for the front door and the carport and the back deck. "I'm turning on all the outside lights. Hopefully that will keep the animals away."

"Get some sleep."

"Yeah, no. Don't think so. My heart is racing a million miles an hour."

"Well, I'm going back to sleep. Hope you can, too."

"Thanks." *I wish you were here*, I almost said. "I'll talk to you soon. Thanks for checking on me."

We said goodbye and I crawled into bed, willing my heart to slow down, and hoping I could go back to sleep. I finally drifted off about four, and my alarm woke me up at six. It was going to be a long, long Tuesday.

I had no new cases that day, but that didn't mean I wasn't busy. I had opened a case on a family two weeks ago that was going downhill, fast. A home visit revealed them to be in constant chaos, with the teen boy and his mother in a constant state of shouting and the elementary school-aged girl, terrified, hiding in the closet to avoid the noise. The mother was about three seconds away from losing control and beating both the kids to a pulp. I sat down with her and was trying to assess whether it was even worth it to try to keep the kids in the home. I decided everybody needed a break and got permission to contact the maternal grandparents in Georgia. Mom worked two jobs, and said she didn't have the time or the money to take them over there, nor a car that would make it. I went back to the office and spent most of the early afternoon on the phone with the grandparents, explaining the situation and asking if the grandkids could come visit for a couple of weeks? They agreed to have me bring them over tomorrow. I phoned the mother and asked them to have them ready at nine. I updated Mac and told him I would be heading to Atlanta the next day. Luckily the alarm on my phone stayed quiet all day.

I picked up LaReesa at the Fowlers after dinner, and we made a short visit to Dad's to pick up my stuff. LaReesa and Dad were happy to see each other, and he agreed to have her come over in the morning. Reese was full of stories about her trip to church on Sunday, and asked if she could go again with them next weekend. I agreed, and told my own news to the two of them.

"Grant and I are going out tomorrow night. On a date."

That got a big smile from Dad, and Reese pumped a fist in the air with a "Yes!"

Dad said, "I wish you luck. Have a great time."

"Can I stay home by myself?" Reese asked.

I looked at Dad. He said, "I have a date with Vicky tomorrow. We are going to out to dinner. Sorry."

"Please?" Reese asked.

"I don't think so, Reese. Not—" I said, as she gave a loud noise of protest, "because of you, but because of that text. Your safety is the most important thing."

"I can take care of myself."

"No doubt, but it would make me feel better if you had someone with you. An adult. Do you think you could stay the night with Sharonda?" I hated to ask the Fowlers to host her again, and made a mental note to buy Cheryl a nice bottle of wine.

"Lemme see." She typed on her cell phone. "Tha' way, if you and Grant wanna get nekkid, I'll be gone."

My father said, "La la la la la."

"Reese! That is not going to happen. And if it did, it's none of your business. N.O.Y.B."

"Why not? Not like y'all ain't done it before."

"N.O.Y.B."

Dad said, "La la la la la" again.

"We are not going to talk about this. Ever. And not in front of my dad."

"Alright. You do you." Her phone pinged and she checked it. "Sharonda said it's fine if I stay over."

I pulled out my cell and called Cheryl. "Hi Cheryl," I said when she answered.

"Damn, you don' believe me?" Reese shrieked.

I held my hand up to signal her to be quiet. "Did Sharonda ask if Reese could stay the night tomorrow?"

"She did. That's fine. She's no problem, really."

"I feel like we have been asking a lot from you recently, and I really appreciate your watching her."

"Sharonda tells me you are going out with Grant, so I'm happy to help."

Dang, my business was all over town. "Thanks. I hope it goes well."

"Me, too," she said. "Are you going to bring her over or do you want me to come get her?"

"I'll bring her over. Is five okay?"

"Perfect."

We disconnected and I told Reese I'd take her over at five tomorrow. She was irked with me all the way home, until she saw the camera in the carport.

"Cool! They let you know when someone is here?"

"Yes, there is a very loud alarm on my phone."

"Guess I can't sneak out no more."

I shot her a look.

"Jus' kiddin'. I ain't sneakin' out."

"You better not be."

I turned on all the lights outside again before we went to bed. Reese cracked up when I told her what happened last night with the racoon. I bid her goodnight and she was still howling with laughter as I pulled her door closed.

Wednesday morning, I dropped off Reese at Dad's and picked up a sullen teenage boy and an excited little girl. It was about two and a half hours of drive time to the part of northwest Atlanta where the children's grandparents lived. I spent a lot of that time explaining to the sulking boy that things better improve at home or we were going to have to find him a new place to live. I made a mental note to follow up on the in-home counseling referral I had made. I dropped the kids off at the grandparents and spent some time hearing about how their mother had run away, pregnant, at age eighteen and, although they were hoping to rebuild a relationship with her and the children, they weren't optimistic.

It took me an extra hour to get out of Atlanta, plus there was a time change, so I got back to Birmingham about four. I had to pick Reese up a few minutes before five and get her to the Fowlers. I remembered to stop by the Piggly Wiggly and get a nice bottle of wine for Cheryl. I went to Dad's, loaded Reese in the car and wished Dad a good time on his date. He said the same.

I dropped Reese off at five minutes after five. Cheryl was grateful for the wine and offered to share it with me, but I didn't have time. I raced home, took a shower, and got myself made-up and changed into a sundress and sandals just as Grant arrived.

He looked amazing, his khaki pants neatly ironed and matched with a light green dress shirt that showed off his eyes. He greeted me with a kiss on the cheek.

Once in the van, I asked, "So where are we going?"

"I made us reservations at Bocca, downtown."

I gave him a wry smile. "Italian food. What a surprise."

"Is that okay? Do you want to go somewhere else?"

"No, no. It's awesome. I've been wanting to try there."

The restaurant was in the Loft District downtown, and decorated in modern, industrial style. The hostess greeted us with, "Hello, Mr. Summerville. Nice to see you again." Grant explained that he had brought prospective clients here a few times. We were shown to a table for two. We both ordered a glass of red wine and studied the menu. We chatted about all the dishes and Grant said the meatballs were fantastic. We ordered and I asked Grant about work.

"We got the contract for the new hospital, so I'm hiring again. Luckily a lot of young adults have just graduated, so I'm getting a lot of applications."

"Congratulations. That is going to be a big job."

"It won't start for a few months, but yeah. What about you? How's work?"

"Busy. It's always busy, as you know."

We were waiting on our entrees when my phone screamed in my purse. Moments after, Grant's phone made a similar noise. I fished it out of my purse, quickly, to stop the noise. Other diners were giving us disapproving glares.

I pulled up the Reolink app and checked the pictures from the cameras.

There was a woman in my carport, and she was picking the lock to the carport door.

"Holy shit," I said. "Can you see this? I'm calling the cops."

"I'm recording the video. Do you want to leave?"

"Of course, if you don't mind."

Grant left some cash on the table for the wines while I dialed 911 and asked for the city of Hoover. I got transferred as we got into the van and I explained that someone was breaking into my home. I gave the address in Bluff Park, on Bedford Avenue. The police were on their way.

Grant raced his van back to my neighborhood and thankfully we did not get pulled over on the way home. The police were still there when we arrived. Two cop cars, lights flashing by the curb. Grant pulled into the driveway and the four officers approached us. They had investigated the outside of the house and found no one there. One of the officers was the same one who had come out a few days ago and knew the story, so it was nice not to have to repeat it. Grant pulled up the video and we looked at it with the officer.

"That's not Regina," Grant and I both said at the same time.

The woman in the video was black. She was stocky, about my age, with lots of hair that was more natural afro than styled. It was streaked with a little gray. She wore black jeans and a loose faded, black t-shirt and apparently had not noticed that she was being filmed.

Officer O'Reilly asked, "You know who she is?"

I answered, "No, I have no idea."

Grant said, "We should ask—"

"Yep."

I looked at Officer Chambers. "I have a foster daughter. I'm calling her now."

I called Cheryl's number and when she answered, I said we had had a break in and I needed to see LaReesa here right away. She offered to bring her home and she said they'd be there in a minute. Officer O'Reilly said we should go in the house and see what was missing. There was a lump of fear in my stomach the size of a boulder as we entered through the carport. Grant took my hand and held it as we toured the house.

I turned on all the lights when we got in. The house was quiet, except for the humming of the air conditioner and the fridge. The television was still there. We walked back to the office, and my laptop was still there. My bedroom was fine. My jewelry box, which was full of nothing but costume stuff that wasn't worth anything, still sat on my dresser. LaReesa's room seemed the same. She and Cheryl and Sharonda pulled up just as we finished looking around. They dropped Reese off, and we greeted her at the front door. She glanced at all of the officers, fear etched on her face.

"You okay?" She asked me.

"I'm fine. Grant and I were at dinner when the alarm went off."

She threw her arms around me in a big hug, which I

returned. Then Grant got one. He said, "We want you to look at a video. We caught the burglar on film." He handed her his cell phone and played the video. Her eyes went wide.

"Oh sh--, I mean, that's my mamma."

Chapter Eleven

"You sure?" Officer Chambers asked.

"Positive. That's her."

"LaReesa," I said, "I need you to go look in your room and see if anything is missing."

LaReesa walked back to her bedroom and I focused on the officer. "Her name is Amara Jones and she just got out of prison in March. I'm sure this is a probation violation and I want to press charges."

He nodded and wrote her name down in his notebook. "Do you have an address for her?"

"She might be living in her parents' old home in Midfield." I recited the address for him. "I'm not a hundred percent sure, but that is the last one I know. She has a long history of drug use and prostitution."

"Is she trying to get her daughter back?"

"No! That's the weird thing. She has filed nothing with Family Court. No request for visitation, custody. Nothing."

Reese came back to the living room. "I think one of my shirts is missin'. You know that cute V-neck blue one I got a month ago? I had it on yesterday?"

I nodded.

"It was on the top of my dirty clothes pile. It's gone."

"You're sure? I don't know how you can find anything in that mess."

"I'm sure. Why the hell would she steal my clothes?"

"I don't know, honey. The police will find her."

"An' then she goin' back to jail, right?"

I glanced at Grant. "Yes, probably. Robbery is a probation violation, so she'll probably go back."

"Dumb ass."

"Language."

"But she is. She probably high, too."

"Well, let's wait and see what the police find out."

We said goodbye and thank you to the police officers. It was now seven-thirty and I was starving. Reese said she had not eaten dinner, yet, either. We discussed where to go.

"I don' wanna mess up yo date," she said.

Grant said, "Oh, we can reschedule. I hope."

I smiled. "Of course we can."

"We could get something to go and I could show you my new house," Grant offered.

Both Reese and I agreed and we climbed into Grant's van. He exited my neighborhood, took a left on Shades Crest Road and we traveled down the mountain. We crossed Highway 150, and from there it was just a mile or so to the entrance to his neighborhood. He made his way through the pleasant residential homes to a little cul-de-sac.

The house was cute. It sat at the far end of the circle and had a large front window with a porch on the side, off the living room. The front door was red, and the house was painted gray with white trim. The shutters were black. Grant parked the van in the driveway and we entered through the front door to face a set of wooden stairs.

"Let's go up first," Grant directed.

We climbed the half-flight of stairs to enter a large living area with a white-tiled fireplace to one side. The walls were a soft white and the hardwood floors were shiny and new. The living room held one folding garden chair and a laptop on a foldable TV tray.

LaReesa laughed. "You ain't got no stuff."

"Well, yeah, not yet. The stuff I had, I sold last year. I've got to go shopping."

He showed us the three bedrooms down a hallway, his king-sized bed in the main one with a set of white sheets and a fuzzy tan blanket on it. All his clothes were still in boxes. The other two bedrooms were empty. The kitchen was nice, and featured a large island and a bay window that overlooked the backyard. Downstairs was a finished basement, filled with trestle tables covered with computers and electronic parts, and another large, empty bedroom with a bathroom.

"It's a great house," I said. "It's so quiet here."

"I really love it," he said. "More than I thought I would."

Grant ordered Chinese food from a place nearby, and while we waited on the delivery, he showed us all the things he had automated so far in the house. A control panel made from a Kindle was mounted on the wall and controlled the lights and the ceiling fans. He said eventually it would control the blinds on the windows, when he got them installed. It made me smile.

"What?" Grant asked.

"It figures you would get everything automated before you even have furniture."

"I do the important stuff first."

The food arrived and we sat in a circle on his living room floor and picnicked with paper plates. We were eating and chatting when we heard a car enter the cul-de-sac. I looked up to see headlights heading for the house. The sedan pulled up to the curb in front of his house and we heard someone get out. It was too dark outside to see many details. Suddenly there was a loud crash and I saw Reese scoot back on her butt as a large rock landed in front of her.

"What the fu--, I mean, what the heck?" LaReesa shrieked.

Grant bolted to the window and began to take pictures with his phone. The car was speeding away but I had time to see that it was a small, white car.

"Watch the glass!" I said to the room as Reese stood up. The large rock had a piece of paper tied to it. Reese reached for it but I stopped her.

"Don't touch anything. Let's let the police pick that up." Grant was dialing 911 on his phone, a rare look of fury on his face.

Once again, the police arrived quickly. Grant went through the story again about Regina and showed them the rock and the large hole in one of the panes of the front window. We gave the rock to the officer, who unfolded the note. Mostly it was profanity, a lot of f-words in a letter about how he "sucks" and "he was going to pay." I found a broom and dustpan and swept up the glass as Grant finished with the officer. After the police left, I put the food away as he found a piece of cardboard and patched the hole in the window. The fury was still visible on his face.

"I'm so sorry," I said.

"This is getting out of hand. I'm going to the police tomorrow and force them to do something. Get a warrant.

Something."

Reese was pacing the room. "I dare her to come here again. I frickin' dare her."

I turned to her. "Once again, this is a matter for the police. We are going to let them handle it."

"Police ain't gon' do nothing. They never do."

I had nothing to say to that, so I asked Grant to drive us home and he agreed. I was a little worried about his staying at his house alone tonight and voiced this to him.

He smiled. "I'll be all right."

We loaded in his van and he drove us home. He walked us both in and checked the house to make sure we were safe before I walked him back out to his van.

"Sorry our dinner got ruined." I said.

"Not your fault. It gives us a chance for a do-over. How about next Friday?"

"That sounds amazing."

He kissed me goodnight, good and proper this time, and when we came up for air he said, "Stay safe. I'll call you tomorrow."

"You too."

Thursday morning, I woke Reese and took her to Dad's. She gave me a lot of grief about the kiss on the way there. "Y'all done be makin' out in the middle of the road. Hoo-ee, that was somethin'!"

"How did you—"

"I was watching out the window."

I gave her a playful slap on the shoulder. "Spyin' on me?"

"Just lookin' out."

I got to work at the same time as Russell, who said he had an appointment with Jerry Cook today at nine a.m. He was coming here, and Russell invited me to sit in, as long as I didn't tell Mac. I had no appointments until the afternoon, so I agreed.

Jerry arrived at quarter to nine and was shown to the meeting room on our floor by Beth. He was an energetic guy, skinny but fit, and dressed in old jeans and an old t-shirt that had several tiny holes in it. His brown hair was receding already. His leg bounced in the chair as we introduced ourselves.

"What's this all about? I've got to get to work." He had a strong southern accent.

"What do you do?" I asked.

"I'm a welder at Eyer Manufacturing."

Russell said, "You dated a girl in high school, Regina Maynard? She had a baby?"

"Dylan. Yeah."

"Are you the father?"

His expression turned sad as he answered, "I don't know. She was sleeping with a lot of other guys. That's why we broke up."

"How many is a lot?" I asked.

He shrugged. "At least two others I know of. One was one of my teammates on the football team, Jackson Davenport. The other was our science teacher, Mr. Almogordo."

"Whoa," I said.

"I know, gross, right? All the girls in the high school had a crush on him. After we broke up, I heard she was bragging about seducing him. She was the one who got him, everyone was saying."

"So you broke up before she got pregnant?" Russell asked.

"When Jackson was bragging in the locker room, that he had slept with her, I confronted her. She admitted it. I ended it, right there. Two months later she calls me to tell me she's pregnant. I asked her who the father was, and she said she had no idea. I told her good luck and that was the last time I talked to her. She's a horrible person, only cares about herself. I'm not surprised she's had DHS called on her."

I asked, "Dylan's middle name is Gerald. Is that your full name, by any chance?"

He looked surprised. "It is. Gerald Andrew Cook the second is my full name. I wonder why she did that?"

"Maybe she still had feelings for you?" Russell asked.

"She can go to hell."

Russ continued, "Has she ever asked you for a paternity test?"

73

"No."

"Would you be willing to take one?"

"Does it cost anything? I ain't got much money."

I glanced at Russell and said, "It may have to be ordered through the courts, if she won't comply, and tests are about three hundred dollars."

"I ain't got near that much money."

I said, "Let's table that for now. We can work something out later if we need to. Did this Mr. Almogordo ever get any consequences for what he did with her?"

Jerry chuckled wryly. "He still teaches at the high school. I heard Regina wasn't the only girl he—you know."

I thought back to Dr. Grace Allen, the principal at the high school. I had a strong feeling that if she even had the slightest suspicion that anything of this nature was going on, she would handle it, and quickly. I voiced this thought.

"Yeah, she was pretty cool, Dr. Allen. I can't imagine what she would do if she had proof. Fire his ass for starters."

"I'm kinda surprised Regina hasn't gone after anyone for child support," I mused out loud. "She always seems to want money."

Jerry answered me. "She'd have to fess up to how many boys she'd had sex with, and that's a high number, I think. She's a slut."

I had nothing to add to that, and glanced at Russell. He asked, "Would you be interested in discovering if you are Dylan's dad? We can help you file the paperwork with the courts."

"Can I think about it? I mean, I'm living with my mom and dad right now because I can't afford a place on my own. My girlfriend and I are trying to save up money for a down payment on some land to build on. I don't know if I can afford a son right now."

"Let's keep in touch and we can revisit all this later." Russ stood up and offered a hand to Jerry, along with a business card. "Thanks for coming in."

Russell walked Jerry out and I returned to our office. Russ joined me a few minutes later. He said, "He seems like a sweet guy."

"Yeah, too bad he landed with her. I want to go talk to Dr. Allen about this Mr. Almogordo."

"Need I repeat Mac's warning? You need to stay out of this case."

"Need I repeat this is for Grant? I still want to help him. You won't say anything, will you?"

"Of course not. Just keep me informed."

I had one other appointment later this afternoon, so needed to get on the road. I bid Russ goodbye and grabbed my stuff and headed for my car. While in my car, I called my best friend, Royanne Fayard, at her office. Royanne and I had lunch every Thursday, unless my crazy schedule prevented it, and it looked like this was one of those days. We agreed to reschedule for later. I was in Hayden in less than an hour and walked in to the office of the high school as I had before, calling hello.

Dr. Allen emerged from her office, today dressed in a cute, lightweight dress which showed off her pretty figure. "Oh, hello again."

"Sorry to disturb, Dr. Allen, but do you have a minute to talk?"

"Sure, come through."

I sat in the same chair I had before and took a deep breath. "I've been looking into Regina Maynard's background. We've talked to Jerry Cook, so thanks for that information. He says that Regina told him she had, um, sexual relations with her science teacher. A Mr. Almogordo?"

I watched as the blood drained from her face and her mouth opened slightly. I continued. "There is some concern that he may be Dylan's father. I wondered if you had any thoughts on that."

She cleared her throat and I could see her pulling herself together mentally. I'd shocked her, for sure. "David Almogordo is a science teacher here, yes. I have never heard any allegations of impropriety against him, before now. He is a very good-looking man, and many of my students do get, crushes on him, for lack of a better word. But I've never heard that he has done anything inappropriate."

"I'd love to talk with him. Do you have a phone number,

or an address where I can reach him?"

"I'm not comfortable releasing that information without talking to him first." She chewed her bottom lip. "And I'm going to have to get my Superintendent involved."

"You are surprised by this."

"David has taught here for nine years. We've never had any issues."

"Will he be fired? If this turns out to be true?"

"Like I said, I have to get my Superintendent involved. A lot of these questions will involve the County office."

"And this is the first you've heard of this?"

"Well, one hears rumors, you know, about his—being friendly with kids. But no one has...this is the first time that someone has made..."

"A direct accusation."

"Yes."

Someone finally said it out loud, I thought. *That's what she's reacting to.*

"If you'll excuse me, I have work to do." Dr. Allen said.

I stood up. "I'll need to talk to him." I retrieved a business card from my purse. "Can you pass on my number, have him call me?"

"I will do that."

"Sorry to be the bearer of bad news," I said with a small grin.

She didn't return the smile. "Have a nice afternoon."

I made my way to my car, checking my watch on the way there. My appointment was in Trussville, on the far east side of Birmingham, in an hour. I made it with a little time to spare and everything went surprisingly well. This was a case I had for a while, and I needed to decide about either closing it or transferring it to another unit. I decided to head back to the office and discuss it with Mac.

I got back to the office at about three-thirty. Mac was in a meeting and I waited to talk to him. When I finally got to speak to speak with him, it was just after four. I updated him about the family in Trussville, and he agreed I could have the case closed. I asked him if he'd been updated by Russell on the latest about Regina.

"I told you to stay out of it."

"I'm not in it." He gave me a skeptical look. "Really. But Russ met with a guy that may be Dylan's father, and he alleges that Regina was sleeping with one of her teachers in high school, as well as one of the football players."

"She really gets around," he said.

"Jerry Cook says he has no idea who Dylan's father is, although Dylan's middle name is Gerald, which is Jerry's full first name."

"How do you know that?"

"I saw Dylan's birth certificate. Russ and I share an office, you know. And we talk."

Mac took a deep breath. I continued. "We gave the name of the teacher to Dr. Allen, and she's investigating and will keep us informed."

"Us? There's really nothing I can say to make you stay out of this case, is there?"I shrugged. "Just helping out."

"Go back to work."

I went back to my office. Russ was gone, and I decided to call it a day. I picked up LaReesa at Dad's and when I got home, Grant's van was parked in front of my house. He was sitting in it, waiting for us. He followed us into the air-conditioned house, an anxious look on his face. LaReesa went to her room, and I asked, "What's up?""Look, I'm gonna have to talk quick. The police want to meet, they want to talk to both of us. We have to go to the station."

"Why?"

"Regina Maynard is dead. Murdered."

Chapter Twelve

"Wait. What?" I could feel my blood rushing to my feet as I slumped onto the sofa.

"The police came to my shop at about three o'clock. Regina's body was found in a lake, off Guyton Road, very close to where I live. Dumped there, they think. She'd been shot."

"Oh, God."

"I told the detectives we would meet them at the station off Valleydale Road at five-thirty." He checked the digital watch on his wrist. "So we have to get going."

I went to LaReesa's room and told her I had an urgent errand to run with Grant, and that I'd be home a little after six-thirty, hopefully. Her gaze was locked on her phone and she grunted and waved a hand at me in response. I had a little concern about leaving her home alone, but there wasn't much I could do about it.

Grant and I got in his van and went to the Hoover Public Safety Center. Hoover is a large city of 92,000 people that spans two counties, and the police station was in Shelby County, south of us and about twenty minutes away. The large, new Center had a front wall of glass and large concrete columns in the front. We entered the station and talked to the officer at the front desk. Two men, one white and one black, came to the desk and introduced themselves as Detectives Graves and Jefferson. Grant and I were separated. He gave me a nervous glance and squeezed my hand before I was shown to a small room with a table and four chairs.

I was with the white detective, Detective Graves, and another man who didn't introduce himself and was apparently there just to take notes. Graves, like most cops I knew, had the air of an ex-military man; his posture was ramrod straight and his dark blond hair cut into a crew cut. His blue suit was neatly pressed. He began, "Thank you for meeting with me. Your name, and Mr. Summerville's, came up in the system when we began investigating this case. He's your boyfriend, correct?"

"Sort of."

"Sort of?"

"We broke up in January. We've been spending a bit of time together recently, because of Regina and all her mess."

He picked up the file and opened it, and I could see the printed copy of the text that Regina had sent Grant last Saturday. Several other copies of police reports were also there. "I understand Mr. Summerville has been having problems with Regina Maynard for quite some time."

I answered, "It's really gotten bad these past two weeks."

"When was the last time you saw Regina?"

"In person, face to face? Hardly ever. She threw a large rock through Grant's window last night as we were having dinner. I assume you have the note that was tied to it?"

The detective studied the papers. "I do."

"She was stealing from Grant, and his clients. She has a history of stealing, even back to her high school days."

The detective's eyes narrowed. "How do you know that?"

I took a deep breath. "Regina Maynard made a false report of child abuse against Grant Summerville. I work for DHS, in the child welfare department, and we have been investigating her case. Where is Dylan, by the way?"

The detective looked alarmed. "Dylan?" he asked.

"Her son. She has a six-year-old son. My colleague and I have been trying to work out where she lives, but have had no luck."

"The address on her Alabama driver's license was an apartment at The Falls and Woods apartments."

"She doesn't live there anymore."

"We know."

"She doesn't live with her parents, either. They live up in Hayden and have told DHS that they haven't seen her in six months."

"I'm going to have to send someone up there to do the notification. Do you have their address?"

"I can probably get it, if I can make a phone call?"

"Make it quick."

I pulled out my cell phone and dialed Russell's number. He answered, "What's up?"

"Hey, I'm with the Hoover police and I can't talk long.

Regina Maynard is dead. Do you know her parent's address, offhand?"

"What? Dead? She's dead?"

"Her body was found in the lake off Guyton Road. Address?"

He told me the address in Hayden, which I repeated as he stated it. The detective wrote it down.

"Are you still at work?"

"Yeah, I am."

"Can you go update Mac? Tell him I'll call him later."

"Will do. Call me later, too, please."

"I will. Bye."

The detective focused on me again. "What makes you sure it was her, last night?"

"We saw her car. A little white Kia Rio."

"We think she was murdered a little after ten this morning. She was shot in the chest and abdomen. The autopsy will be done Monday, at the coroner's office."

I asked, "Do you know where she was murdered?"

He thought for a moment before answering me. "We think it had to have been close to where she was dumped, but we don't know the exact location. We got a search warrant for Mr. Summerville's house and that's being executed as we speak."

"What? Now?"

"Yes, now."

"But Grant didn't kill Regina. He wouldn't do that."

"But he does own a gun. One he bought recently."

I could feel the blood rushing to my feet again. "He bought one because she threatened him. Many times. And we called the police every time it happened."

"Where were you at ten a.m., yesterday?"

"At work. I was doing an interview with my coworker, Russell DePaul. Do you need his number?" The man taking notes passed me a pen and a sheet of paper, and I wrote down Russ's number.

Detective Graves pulled a radio out of his pocket and left the room. I sat there, in the still, quiet room, and waited with the other man, who didn't say anything. I wondered where

Grant was. I looked around the room and noticed the small camera mounted in the corner, recording everything. The detective came back and sat across from me, again.

"Do you have any idea who may have murdered Miss Maynard?" he asked.

"I have no idea. She has a history of pissing people off, though." I told him about her history at Grandma's Apron, and what she had done to poor Henrietta and Fred Maple. The other guy continued to take notes.

I also relayed the allegations of her sleeping with her high school science teacher. I hoped the police would give Dr. Allen time to handle that on her end. No doubt it would be common knowledge soon enough. Detective Graves thanked me for my time and showed me back out to the lobby after handing me a card and asking me to call if I thought of anything else.

"Will there be an AMBER Alert put out for Dylan?"

"We have no evidence he's in immediate danger. She probably just left him with a friend, or a boyfriend. I'm sure he'll turn up, but we will be looking for him."

It was my turn to hand him a business card. "Will you call me directly, when you find him? I'd like to handle his case personally."

"Sure."

Grant joined us, escorted to the lobby by the other Detective, Jefferson. Grant looked pale and tense. We bid the officers goodbye and went to his van. He sat in the driver's seat a minute, collecting himself.

"That was awful," he said. He was shaking a bit, and I reached over and put my hand on his shoulder. "They said I have motive, and a weapon. They are going to call my employees and make sure I was at work today. They said I was mad about her throwing the rock through my window, so I killed her. And they searched my house. It's ridiculous."

"I know. They told me. They won't find anything."

"This is a nightmare."

I squeezed his shoulder and gave him a small smile. "Why don't you come hang out at my house for a bit? We could watch a movie or something, get our minds off this."

He nodded and cranked the van. We made our way up Highway 31 to Patton Chapel Road and from there to Bluff Park. The sun was just disappearing as we pulled up to my house.

Another car was parked at the curb, an older, silver Chevy. I unlocked the front door and went into the living room. I heard a giggle from LaReesa's room. I gave Grant a look and we walked down the hall to her door.

I opened the door to see a large, moving lump under the comforter on the bed. I heard Reese say, "Oh, shit," and then she and the boy sat up.

Chapter Thirteen

I was suddenly hit with an intense rage that flooded my body. "Who the hell are you?" I shouted.

The young black man was still wearing navy basketball shorts, thank God. He threw back the bedclothes and stood up, scanning the room for his t-shirt. He found it on the floor and put it on. "I'm Devin," he said. He was a good-looking young man, muscular, with his short hair neatly cut around his dark-skinned face.

LaReesa was in her bra, and scrambling around in the bed looking for her shirt. She tried to keep the comforter pulled up over her top so we couldn't see anything.

"How old are you?" I asked.

"I'm eighteen."

"Well, Devin, LaReesa, who is thirteen by the way, is not allowed to have anyone over when I am not home, so I'm going to need you to leave."

Grant's six-foot-five frame stood tall behind me. "Now." He said it in an intense tone I had never heard him use before. It scared me a bit.

Devin said, "Yes, sir," and walked out the door. Grant followed him. I heard the front door open and shut.

I was so mad at her I couldn't speak. I walked out to the living room as I heard the Chevy drive away. I turned on the lamps in the living room and LaReesa, now fully dressed, joined me and Grant. She turned on me.

"Damn, I wasn't gonna fuck him!" she shouted. "Why you gotta barge in here and be all up in my business?"

"It sure as hell looked like you were about to fuck him!" I shouted. "In your bed and half dressed!"

"I'm on the pill!"

"That does not constitute permission!"

I stopped and took a deep breath. Yelling and cussing at her wasn't going to help the situation. "Give me your phone."

"What? Oh, come on!"

"You have broken the rules, and you will get it back in two weeks. Or shall I have it disconnected altogether? I can do that, you know."

She stormed back to her room and brought me the iPhone, cased in an orange-patterned case. She slapped it in my hand so hard it stung, then stormed back to her room. The door slammed, and I could hear her cussing me behind it.

Grant had stood silently, watching us. "Well done," he said to me, quietly.

I looked at him. "What?"

"You got ahold of your temper and gave her an appropriate consequence for her behavior."

"I wanna kill her."

He chuckled. "I know, but think of it from her point of view. Her mother is out of prison and broke in here and stole her stuff. She's stressed."

"I don't care. That's not a good reason to do what she did."

He walked over and wrapped his arms around me. I felt myself melt into his embrace as I said, "It's just such a struggle, trying to keep her away from drugs and prostitution. Those two things were all she saw, growing up. She knows they will get her attention. And money."

"It's going to take time."

"I know."

I made us some tacos for dinner, but Reese refused to come out of her room and join us. Fine, I thought. Stay in there and be mad.

After dinner, Grant and I went out to the back deck to sit and talk. The heat had finally moderated now that it was after nine p.m. and we sat and enjoyed the quiet darkness. I took a deep breath. "God, what a day."

"It has been a chaotic one, for sure."

"Are you going to call your attorneys? I mean, the trial is off now."

"Yeah, that's on my list of things to do tomorrow."

"I guess that's a relief, no?"

"I mean, it is. I am sorry she is dead. As nice as it is that the trial is cancelled, I wouldn't wish anybody dead."

"Oh, I know. I'm just so worried about little Dylan. I hope they can find him, and that she hasn't sold him."

"Sold him?"

"Child trafficking. It happens more than you think."

"Good God."

"Sometimes He's not," I scoffed.

"Are you still mad at Reese?"

"I mean, I am. I'm having second thoughts about taking her phone away for so long. But it's the best consequence for her actions. It gets her attention. But you're right. Having her mom appear after so long is bound to affect her behavior. I'll go talk to her in a bit."

We sat, enjoying the silence for a while, until he said, "I guess I better go. If I sit here much longer, I'm not going to be able to peel myself out of this chair."

I'd thought about asking him to stay over, but I had work in the morning and it was nearly ten o'clock. I was exhausted, and needed to go to sleep. I walked him to the door and he gave me a sweet kiss goodnight. "I'll call you tomorrow," I told him.

After he drove away, I retrieved Reese's cell phone from my room and knocked on her door.

"What?" she snapped.

"I want to talk to you."

"Come in then."

She sat on her bed, her back against the wall, fuming at me. I joined her there. I was a little surprised there wasn't rap music blaring, but then I remembered that was on her phone, too.

"Look," I said. "It's been a long, rough week. I get that. And having your mom come back has been stressful. Sometimes it's hard to know what to do with those feelings."

The tears welled and started falling from her eyes. "I jus' wanted to have some fun and relax and forget about things for a while."

"But there's other ways to do that, other than sex."

"I tol' you, I wasn't going to have sex with him."

"Okay, but you were partially undressed, and in bed with him. That can lead to, you know, things."

"I told him no."

"But what if he didn't listen? What if he had raped you? We weren't home, and nobody would have heard you if you

87

cried for help. I just worry about you, that's all."

"I can take care of myself." She wiped the tears from her face.

"No doubt. You are very good at that. Maybe it's time, though, to let some adults take care of you."

The tears increased, and I reached over and stroked her arm. "Let me do that, okay?"

"What if she files for custody? What if she makes me come live with her? I don't want to. I like it here."

"She can't make you do anything. It's up to the Court. And so far, she has not shown any indication that she is going to file for custody. And if she does, I'm going to fight her in court. I don't want you to leave, either."

She fell into my arms, sobbing, and wrapped her arms around my neck. I let her stay there, and cry for a while, before we broke apart. "Let me do the worrying, okay?"

She nodded and wiped her nose with her hand. I pulled her phone out of my pocket. "Here. You can have this back. But no boys over when I'm not home, or I really will take it away."

"Thanks."

"Get some rest. I've got work tomorrow and you are going to Dad's."

She nodded again and I left her in her room with some tissues. I got ready for bed and lay there for a while, thinking. I fell asleep thinking of little Dylan, wondering where he was. And what DHS would do with him if he turned up.

Friday morning arrived too soon. I dragged myself out of bed and roused Reese, who was also sleepy and had swollen eyes. I dropped her off at Dad's and filled him in on all that had happened yesterday. He agreed he and Reese would take it easy today.

I got to work and checked my schedule. It was nearly the weekend, and I hadn't scheduled much for today, just a couple of home visits in the early afternoon. Russell struggled in at eight-thirty and I apologized for not calling him last night. I explained everything that had happened yesterday, including Reese's activities. Mac appeared in the doorway as I was telling the story, and demanded to see us both in his office. Once there, I had to go through the whole thing again.

"So we have no idea where this kid Dylan is?" Mac asked.

"I asked the police if they were going to put out an AMBER Alert, but the officer said there is no evidence that he has been abducted or is in immediate danger. They seem to think he will turn up."

"Let's hope so."

I continued, "He's likely with a friend of hers, or a boyfriend. Russ updated you on his meeting with Jerry Cook?"

"Mmm." Mac grunted. "Though it seems Jerry is only one of a number of possible fathers. I wish we had more info, for when Dylan shows up." Mac looked at Russell and asked, "Would the grandparents in Blount County be willing to take him?"

"I haven't had that conversation with them yet. I'm headed up there this morning to check in with them. They seem very kind, but are pretty impoverished. I think they would take him, if they can afford it."

"Get up there and see what's up. I'll check in with you later."

We were dismissed, that was clear. Once back in our cubicle, I gave Russ a pleading look with a small smile.

"Don't you have your own cases?"

"My first appointment is at one."

"Will you drive?"

"Sure."

We climbed into my little white Civic and I headed for I-65 north. Russ gave me directions which led us through downtown Hayden and up into the hills beyond the town. I pointed out Grandma's Apron to Russ as we drove by it. We traveled to a large piece of property with an unpaved, dirt road which led to a clapboard house that had to have been at least seventy years old. It was one story, faded brown, with peeling paint and rickety steps that led to the front door. A dilapidated Jayco Hummingbird camper stood next to it, its outdoor skin bent in a couple of places. Russ knocked on the screen door.

The woman that answered was not that much older than me. Her hair was jet black, touched throughout with strands of gray. Her t-shirt was a faded light blue that once had read something I could no longer make out.

"Mrs. Maynard? It's me, Russell DePaul, from DHS?"

"I 'member you."

"This is my colleague, Claire Conover." I nodded a hello.

"Can we come in?"

"Sure." She opened the screen door wide and let us through. The door opened to a living room that was on the small side with what appeared to be the original hardwood floors. They were worn and creaked as we walked across them. The furniture was old, too, but clean. A narrow hallway led to the rooms beyond. A window unit struggled, hard, to combat the heat.

"Ryan's aroun' here someplace."

Russ and I sat next to each other on the sofa while Mrs. Maynard perched in a rickety chair across from us. I said, "I'm so sorry about Regina."

"The cops came up here and tol' us she was dead. Somebody kilt her." Her eyes were focused on the floor in front of us. "They said they was working on finding out who done it. They said Dylan is missin'. They wanted to know if she had a boyfriend or anything, but we ain't got no idea. Ain't seen her since Christmas."

"I'm sure this is very hard for you," Russ said.

She nodded as we heard someone begin to walk towards us from the hall. A man entered the room. He was tall and muscular, and had dark brown hair. He nodded to me and Russell. "Hey."

"Hello, Mr. Maynard. This is my coworker, Claire. Can you join us for a bit?"

Ryan Maynard stepped forward and shook both our hands. His hand was calloused and strong, and he was dressed in jeans and a white t-shirt.

"Not working today?" Russ asked him.

"Naw. Mr. Armstrong done gave me a couple days off, cause of what happened. I got to go back soon, though. We need the money."

"What do you do, Mr. Maynard?" I asked.

"I work for Joe Armstrong, at Armstrong Farms, up in Cullman County. I've worked there since I's fifteen."

"That's hard work," I said.

He nodded. "It's peach harvest season, now, so he needs me."

Russell said, "So the police told you Dylan is missing?"

"They said he most likely with one a Regina's friends. They seem to think he'll show up, somewhere."

"Would you be willing to care for him, when he returns?" Russ asked.

The Maynards shared a glance. Ryan said, "I mean, we got room for him, and he's the last part of our daughter, so, yeah. We was never able to have no more children, other than Regina."

"Thank you for being willing to care for him," I said.

Mr. Maynard spoke again. "Heather and me, we was always willin'. We done bought that camper out there for Regina and him, when he was born. She said she weren't gonna live there, though. Wanted somethin' nicer. We done kept it all these years, hopin' she'd change her mind. Guess we can sell it now." His eyes filled with tears. Mrs. Maynard stood and went over and wrapped her arm around her husband's waist. He kissed her on the temple as he gathered himself. "Sorry," he said.

"Don't apologize," I said. "You both have been through an unimaginable tragedy."

Mrs. Maynard asked, "Do y'all know of anybody that helps with funeral expenses? We're gonna have her cremated, cause it's cheaper, but it's still pricey. I mean, you know, once they release her to us."

I glanced at Russ. He said, "Do you belong to a church? I'd start there."

"We ain't been to church in a couple years, but I can call 'em. Guess we need someone to do the service, too."

I added, "I'd call the county. They have a program where they will bury her, or cremate her—"

"I ain't gonna put her in the county cemetery," Ryan said. "We don't need no charity."

"But they can help you. At least call them."

Russell and I stood and thanked them both for seeing us today. We all agreed to contact each other if we got any word about Dylan.

Back in my car, with the air cranked all the way up, I said, "They are really sweet people."

"Salt of the earth, but poor as hell. Ryan told me his great-grandfather built that house in 1946, and it's been in his family ever since. I guess Dylan will live there someday."

"If he's alive."

"What the hell does that mean?"

"Think about it. His mother was shot. If he was there when it happened…If he saw…We just may not have found his body yet."

Chapter Fourteen

"Christ!" Russell exclaimed. "I mean, I hadn't even thought about that."

"I hope it's not true. I hope he is alive and hasn't been sold to some traffickers."

"Damn, you go to some very dark places."

"Don't you? You work in the same side of the world that I do."

"I try very hard not to."

"Well," I said, "at least we know Dylan has a home when he turns up."

"Right? They are so sweet. I wonder what made Regina so difficult."

"I get her obsession with money, now."

"True. She grew up with not much of anything, so I can see where the greed comes from. You know, Heather had Regina when she was eighteen, just after she and Ryan got married."

"And that's a year older than Regina was when she had Dylan."

"What a cycle."

I dropped Russell off at the office and went to my first appointment. On the way, my phone rang. It was Grant.

"Hey, how's your day going?" he asked.

"You know, so far so good. No emergencies. What about you?"

"Steady. Busy. You doing anything tonight?"

"Just hanging out with Reese. Why?"

"I was hoping we could get some dinner. Reese is invited, too."

"That sounds fun. Then maybe a movie at my house?"

"Perfect. Pick you up at six-thirty?"

"See you then."

My appointment went as well as it could have, and when I was finished, it was close to three. I called Jessica to tell her I was done for the week and then I headed to Dad's. He and Reese were sitting in the living room, watching TV. I was glad to see that they had been taking it easy. I pulled Dad aside to ask how Reese had been doing, and he said they had talked a bit about her mom and she seemed to be dealing with it okay today, meaning no tears. On the way home, I told her Grant had asked us out.

"Cool! Can we get Mexican food?"

"I don't see why not."

I slid on a clean dress when we got home, and Grant arrived precisely at six-thirty. He looked very handsome in a navy polo and the usual khaki pants. Reese had dressed up, too, and looked nice in a tunic and some bright patterned tights. She repeated her request for Mexican food and Grant said that sounded good to him.

We decided on La Brisa and got a table for three fairly quickly. The restaurant was crowded and loud. We had just ordered and were nibbling on chips and salsa when my phone rang.

"Hey you." It was Leah Knighton, who ran the night unit at work. A phone call from Leah was never good news.

"Hang on a sec," I said to her, and indicated to Grant and Reese I had to take this call. I went out the front door of the restaurant to escape the noise. Once on the sidewalk outside, I asked, "What's up?"

"Got a kid here who was just dropped off. Russell's the case worker but he's not answering his phone. Mac said to call you."

"Who is it?"

"Says his name is Dylan Maynard."

"Who dropped him off?"

"I asked him that, and he just shrugged."

"Don't lose him. I'm on my way in."

I went back into the dining room and told Grant and Reese I had an emergency at work. Grant said he could take Reese home after dinner and asked if I needed a ride, since we had taken his van to La Brisa. I told him I would take an Uber so they could enjoy their dinner. Grant said he'd bring my food home.

I logged on to the Uber app and had a ride there within minutes. In the car on the way to the office, I called Detective Graves.

"Dylan Maynard just showed up at the DHS office downtown. I'm on my way there and should be there in about 20 minutes. Can you meet me there?"

"Yep."

"Come to the back door and tell the guard you need to see the night unit."

"Gotcha."

I found Leah in her office. Little Dylan sat on a plastic chair next to her desk. Today's t-shirt had whales on it, and was paired with blue and green plaid shorts. He wore black, velcroed sandals and still needed a haircut. His blue eyes met mine when I stood in the door to the room.

I motioned for Leah to join me in the hallway, and then asked her to go the door and wait for Detective Graves from the Hoover police while I talked to Dylan.

"Detective? Why? What's up?"

"Dylan's mother was murdered this week. That body that was dumped in Guyton Lake? That was his mom."

"Oh, jeez. Poor kid. Should I keep calling Russell?"

"Just leave him a message that says I've got this handled, please."

"Will do."

She walked toward the back door and I focused on Dylan again. "Hey, do you remember me?"

"You're Mr. Grant's girlfriend."

Close enough. "That's right. Do you remember that room you drew pictures in, with Mr. Russell, the last time you were here?"

He nodded, and I asked, "Would you like to go in there and play some more?"

He nodded again and I walked him past the back door, where Leah was chatting with Joel, the security guard. I told her we'd be in the assessment room and led Dylan to that side of the building. I unlocked the door and turned on the lights.

He stood in the doorway, quietly looking around, as I went over and sat on the foam puzzle-mat on the floor. I asked him to join me, and he sat in front of me, legs criss-crossed, and began to pick at a strap on his shoe.

"Listen, I need to tell you something. About your mom."

"She's dead."

"How do you know that?"

"I heard it on the news. Mr. Lonnie didn't know I was listening in kitchen when he was watching the news. Anyway, I saw the blood." His gaze was locked on the floor.

"Dylan, there is a detective on his way here, now. Do you know what a detective does?"

"They solve mysteries, right?"

"Yes! Exactly. See, what happened to your mom is a mystery, and Detective Graves is trying to find out what happened to her."

"You mean who killed her."

"Yes. Do you think you could talk to Detective Graves? He's very nice and wants to find out who did this to her. He is going to need to hear about the blood."

I could sense him withdrawing and I hoped the detective would get here soon. "Would it help you to draw while you talk to him? It might help you explain."

He shrugged and we stood up just as someone knocked on the door. I told Dylan I'd be right back and opened the door to find Leah and Detective Graves standing there. I went into the hallway with them and closed the door behind me as Leah left.

"How is he?" the detective asked.

"Looks shut down. Traumatized. He mentioned a Mr. Lonnie and seeing blood. I thought I'd leave the follow-up to you."

"Can I talk to him alone?"

"Sure. I'll be next door, and I'll be recording this."

"Great, thanks."

"Let me introduce you." I opened the door to see Dylan sitting in one of the chairs at the table, staring at the crayons which stood in a box by his left hand.

"Dylan? This is the detective I was telling you about."

"You can call me Reed," Detective Graves said.

"He wants to talk to you, but I'll be right next door, okay?"

"Okay. Where am I going to live, since my mom is dead?"

"I have met your grandparents up in Hayden, and they

said they hoped you come live with them. Would that be okay?"

He said, "My mom didn't like them. She said they were poor and dumb."

"I didn't get that impression. They seem to love you. I'm going to let Detective Reed take over now, and I'll see you in a bit."

I went to the room next door and, in the darkness, turned on the camera. I faced the mirror and watched.

Detective Graves sat across from Dylan and handed him a piece of paper from the stack on the table. "Thanks for talking to me, Dylan. Do you know what happened to your mom?"

"She's dead."

"How do you know that?"

"I saw it on the news. Mr. Lonnie didn't know I was in the kitchen and could see the TV."

"Who's Mr. Lonnie?"

"Mom's boyfriend."

"Is that where you've been this week? With him?"

"Yeah."

"Miss Claire said you saw some blood?"

Dylan nodded. "When we got home on Thursday. Mr. Lonnie opened the door and there was blood all over the floor by the front door. Some on the walls, too."

"Do you know what time you got home?"

"In the afternoon, after lunch."

"Then what happened?"

"Mr. Lonnie told me to go to my room and don't come downstairs no matter what. So I did. He let me come downstairs that night and the blood was all gone, and the house smelled like bleach."

"Where had you been that day, with Mr. Lonnie?"

"We went to Home Depot, then to the Tractor Supply Store. He was going to buy me a chicken, but they didn't have any."

"Do you know where Mr. Lonnie lives?"

"On a lake. I wanted to swim in it but Mom said no."

"Did the police come to your house?"

"They knocked on the door that night. Mr. Lonnie said

not to answer it and he wasn't going to talk to--"

"To who?"

Dylan squirmed, uncomfortable, before answering his question.

"The goddamn police."

Chapter Fifteen

"I see," Detective Graves said. "Do you know Lonnie's last name?"

"No."

"Can you tell me what Lonnie looks like?"

"He's about my mom's age, I guess. A little older."

"What color hair does he have?"

"Brown, like mine."

"What color are his eyes?"

"Blue."

Interesting, I thought. All the same features as Dylan. And Regina, for that matter. I wondered again about Dylan's paternity.

"Can you tell me anything else about what he looks like?"

"He's got tattoos everywhere. He's got a big one of a tiger, right here," Dylan pointed to his chest, "and L O V E and H A T E on his fingers. I asked him if they hurt, and he said no. He was too tough for them to hurt."

"Do you know how long he was your mom's boyfriend?"

Dylan shrugged. "I don't know. We moved there when I got out of school this year."

"So at the end of May, then?"

"Yes."

"Do you know how they met, your mom and Lonnie?"

"Mom said they met at a bar. She said they really loved each other."

"I wonder why he didn't want to talk to the police."

"Because of his pa—pa something."

"Parole?"

"That's it."

"Do you know why he was on parole?"

"No. Does that have something to do with prison? Mom said he was in prison once. She never told me how come."

"Yes, exactly. Parole is what happens when you get out of prison. Thanks for sharing all this information. How are you feeling?"

Dylan showed no real reaction to the question, merely staring straight at the table. "I'm tired," he said quietly.

"When was the last time you slept?"

"Like, maybe, night before last? Where is my mom?"

"You mean…"

"Her body. Her spirit is in Heaven. That's what Mr. Lonnie said."

"That's right. Her body is with the coroner. He's the man who helps the police after someone is murdered. The coroner will help us investigate. Eventually, we will release your mom's body to her parents and they will have a funeral."

"Can I go home now?"

"I just have a couple more questions, okay? We think your mom was killed in the morning on Thursday. Do you know what her plans were on Thursday?"

"She was gone a lot of the night before. Mr. Lonnie was really mad at her when she got home. Said she didn't need to be out all night partying when she had a kid to take care of."

"So he was babysitting you?"

"Uh-huh."

'Did he ever leave you alone?"

"I don't think so. Me and him watched some cartoons and then we both went to bed. I wanted to sleep in his bed 'cause I was scared but he said no and he made me sleep in my bed upstairs. Is Mr. Lonnie in trouble?"

"I don't know yet, Dylan. I need to talk to him, though. Thanks so much for talking with me."

Dylan answered by giving a big yawn. I left the camera recording and went to the assessment room. "Hey, Dylan, let's go talk to Miss Leah again, okay?"

He nodded and I walked him over to her office and asked him to stay with her was while I finished talking to the detective. I went back to the assessment room and asked Detective Graves to join me in the room next door.

I stopped the camera, logged onto the system at the computer, and asked Detective Graves for his email address. He gave me one that ended in hooveralabama.gov and I emailed him a copy of the file of his interview with Dylan. I also wrote down the address for Ryan and Heather Maynard in Blount County for him, and explained that my next move was to take Dylan up there, after I fetched my car.

"Where's your car?"

"At my house in Bluff Park."

"I'm going back to Hoover, so I can run you both over there."

"Thanks, I'd be really grateful."

I wrote down the Maynard's phone number below their address, then gathered Dylan and we climbed into the Detective's SUV. The ride home at nine at night took a mere fifteen minutes and he dropped us off at the curb in front of my house, behind Grant's van, and bid us good night.

"This is your house?" Dylan asked.

"It is."

"You live here by yourself?"

"No, I have a foster daughter."

"What's a foster daughter?"

"It's a girl I'm taking care of because her parents can't take care of her."

"Why not?"

"Oh, lots of reasons. You want to meet her?"

"Okay."

I opened the carport door. I looked over the dining table to the living room to see Grant and Reese watching TV together on the couch. Grant paused it when the door opened, and they both stood up and faced us.

"Dylan, you remember Mr. Grant? Your mom used to work for him?"

Dylan nodded and said hi. "And this is LaReesa, my foster daughter. Can y'all keep an eye on him for a second while I make a phone call?"

They agreed and I stepped back to the carport, leaning my butt against my Civic and dialing the Maynards on my cell phone. A sleepy Ryan Maynard answered. I explained that Dylan had shown up at DHS and could I bring him home? I could be there in about an hour. He agreed and said they would have his room ready for him.

When I went back in the house, Dylan was sitting on the couch with Reese and she was showing him some part of some game on her phone. I said we needed to go and he handed the phone back to her.

"Take care, Little Man," Reese said. "You in good hands."

"I'll be back in about two hours," I said to Grant, then Dylan and I headed out. He fell sound asleep in the back seat of my car on the way there. We got to the Maynard's about ten-thirty, and Ryan Maynard came out to the car and lifted sleeping little Dylan into his arms as if he weighed nothing. I followed them into the house and down the hallway, whispering to Ryan that I needed to see where he would sleep. He led me to a narrow room next to the bathroom with white walls that were slightly dim with age. A twin bed on a plain metal frame sat in the corner with a worn, orange blanket on it and white sheets. An old wooden dresser was next to it, and that was everything in the room. Ryan tenderly tucked Dylan in and kissed him on the forehead.

He pulled the door nearly closed behind us as Heather joined us in the hall. She was in her nightgown under a stringy, white, terrycloth robe that was tied around her waist. "Is he okay?" she asked.

"He seems physically fine, but upset about his mom."

"Poor baby."

"Can I come back up here tomorrow? I can bring you some clothes and things for him, if you need them? I can fill you in on all that's happened, then."

Heather and Ryan shared a look. I was afraid they'd be too proud to accept my help of clothes and things, and I held my breath while I waited for an answer.

Ryan said, "We'd appreciate that, just to tide us over."

"I'll see you tomorrow afternoon, then."

I yawned the whole way home, interrupted only by the loud growling of my stomach. I got home about midnight and Grant was asleep on the couch, his socked feet hanging over the armrest on one end. He snored softly. I retrieved my dinner from the fridge and was shoving cold bites of burrito in my mouth in the kitchen when he appeared in the doorway.

"Sowwy. 'Id I wak oo?" I said with a mouthful of food.

He chuckled. "It's okay. I'm glad you're home. Reese is asleep. Everything okay with Dylan?"

I swallowed and nodded. "He's with his grandparents."

"I guess I'll head home."

"Don't." I said, impulsively. "I mean, it's really late, and you should just sleep here."

"I don't think my back can take any more time on that couch."

"I didn't mean on the couch. I have to say, though, I'm really exhausted, and I just want to sleep. I don't want you to, I don't know, get your hopes up. Not for tonight."

He leaned over and kissed the top of my head. "I'm going to bed."

I finished the burrito and threw the foam container away. I briefly glanced through the mail on the counter and noted it was nothing that couldn't wait until tomorrow. I brushed my teeth and put on my pajamas and quietly crept into bed. Grant was already asleep, on his side, his brown curls over his eyes. He was snoring softly again. I kissed him gently on his cheek and watched him sleep for a while, thinking, *This. This is what I want forever.* Then I drifted into a deep sleep.

Chapter Sixteen

Saturday morning, I woke up and glanced at the digital clock on the nightstand. Seven. Grant's arms were around me and I snuggled into the warmth of his body and fell back asleep until nine-thirty. The second time I awoke, Grant was gone, but I could hear him and Reese talking in the kitchen. The smell of sizzling bacon was in the air.

I found the two of them cooking breakfast together. Grant was frying eggs on the stove and Reese was draining the bacon I had smelled. "That smells amazing," I said as I reached for a coffee cup and the full pot in the coffee maker.

"We figured after a dinner of cold burrito, you might want a nice hot breakfast," Grant said, leaning to kiss me on the cheek.

"I'm so grateful. Thank you both."

We sat at the dining room table as we ate, and Grant asked what I was up to today. "I need to go shopping," I stated. I explained that I needed to get some clothing and basic supplies for Dylan.

"Can I go?" Reese asked. "It's time to start shopping for clothes for school."

I laughed. "Is it? I guess we are only about six weeks out."

"Can I? I mean, I'm startin' high school. I gotta look right."

"Yes, you can come with me. You can get three outfits to start with, and we'll do some more shopping closer to the actual date."

"Yes!" Reese pumped a fist in the air and looked at Grant. "You coming with us?"

"No, I'm afraid not. My house is a wreck after the police searched it. I need to go check on things there. I was hoping you two would help me furniture shop this weekend?"

"Can we?" LaReesa asked me.

"I've got a busy day today. Maybe tomorrow?" I asked.

"That works for me." Grant said.

We finished breakfast and got ready for the day. Grant kissed me goodbye and said he'd call me later, and Reese and

I climbed into my Civic and headed for the Kohl's department store, down the mountain.

Once in the car, I asked, "Are you nervous about starting high school?"

"Yeah, like, a little. That's a big-ass school, you know? My teacher told me they have like three thousand students."

"They do, but it's a good school. You'll mostly be with your grade, so it won't feel like three thousand."

"I hope not."

"And Sharonda will be there."

"True."

"And you have other friends, right?"

"A couple. There's this girl, Ella, and she pretty cool. We ate lunch together, some. She white, too."

I breathed in a small sigh of relief. I was worried about her adjusting to school in general, and it was nice to hear she was thinking about, and possibly looking forward, to going back. I said, "This is the year where your grades really start to count, you know, if you want to go to Cosmetology School."

"Or Culinary School? Could I go to Culinary School?"

I smiled. "Honey, you can do whatever you decide to do. It's just going to take you putting in the effort, staying out of trouble, and graduating from high school."

We arrived at Kohls and LaReesa skipped in ahead of me and headed to the young women's section. I went to the kids' department and began to look through shirts and shorts for boys. The summer stuff was fairly picked over and it was hard to find much. I found two t-shirts with comic book characters on them and found Reese to see what she thought.

"Spider-man. Yeah, that's cool."

"What about this other one? I don't even know what this is."

"That's Minecraft. A lot of the geeky kids are into that."

I had no idea whether Dylan was a geeky kid or not. I doubted he'd played many video games while he was with his mother, and knew he wouldn't with his grandparents.

LaReesa found two outfits that she liked and tried them on as I waited outside the dressing room. They were both pretty, and miraculously not low-cut or inappropriate. I complemented her on her choices.

"By now, I know the deal."

We went next door to Target where I found a few more shirts and shorts for Dylan, as well as some underwear and shampoo and soap. Reese looked through the young women's section and found some shirts she liked. I made her narrow it down to two and paid for everything.

As we walked out of the store, she asked, "Will you get reimbursed for Dylan's stuff?"

"I'll turn in the receipt and see what happens."

"Do you get reimbursed for my stuff?"

"I probably could, but luckily, I can afford you. So far," I joked.

"Thanks for the clothes. Hope my damn mom doesn't come steal them."

"Any word from her?"

"I ain't heard nothing."

"That's good, right?"

"I guess. I wish I knew what she was plannin' on doing. 'Sides gettin' high."

"Hey, I thought you were going to let me worry about that."

"I can't help it, sometimes."

Damn you, Amara, for putting this kid through this, I thought. I put my arm around her and gave a little squeeze. That reminded me, I needed to follow up with the police next week and see if charges had been filed in the theft from my home.

"I have to go to Blount County to deliver all this to Dylan and his family, okay?"

"Okay. Can Sharonda come over this afternoon? She still wants to walk even though it's a million damn degrees out here."

"Yes, of course she can."

"Can she spend the night?" She asked, taking her cell phone out of her back pocket.

"I don't see why not, if it's okay with her mom."

Cheryl gave permission on the way north, and we reached Blount County about one o'clock. Reese was right, it felt like a million damn degrees outside. The Maynard's window unit was blowing cool air at full speed as I introduced Reese. Dylan came down the hall in the clothes he had worn yesterday and greeted Reese with a small wave. I handed Heather the bags from Kohls and Target.

"Here's some clothes and stuff for Dylan." I smiled at him. "Reese helped me pick it out. I hope you like it."

An overall sense of sadness just emanated from the poor kid. "Thank you," he muttered.

"No problem. You settling in here okay?"

"Yes."

"Can I talk to your grandma for a second?"

"Why don't you show me your room?" LaReesa asked. The two of them went back down the hall.

"How was last night?

"Good, he just slept. We all did, and woke up late."

"I'm going to work on getting him a referral to a grief counselor up here, if that's okay?"

She nodded. "It would be better if it was close, if possible. We ain't got the best transportation and the gas is expensive."

I nodded. "I will do my best. Do you need anything else?"

She shook her head.

"Okay, I'm going to schedule a court date Monday. That's so you can get custody of Dylan. I'll need you to sign some paperwork in the coming days."

"Okay."

I called to Reese to come back in and we said goodbye to Heather and Dylan. I wondered where Ryan was and hoped he was at work, earning money.

Once in the car, LaReesa said, "Dang, that poor kid don't have no toys at all."

"They don't have a lot of money, and they've only had him for one night so far."

"I didn't have no toys when I was a kid, neither. My momma spent all the money on drugs."

"That's sad."

"She wouldn't even buy me nothin' at the dollar store. Every damn dime went to drugs."

"It's okay to be mad at her."

"I know. I am."

We got home about quarter to three and Sharonda was dropped off by Cheryl at three, as scheduled. Reese and Sharonda were both appropriately dressed in shorts, t-shirts, and tennis shoes and they walked off toward the Piggly Wiggly. I watched them from the window as they walked away, both scrolling on their phones as they walked and talked.

I thought about the week ahead, made a grocery list and checked my schedule for the next week. The girls were gone for over an hour, and just as I was beginning to wonder where they might be, I heard screaming.

Chapter Seventeen

I walked out the front door to see LaReesa and Sharonda in the road two doors down. A decades-old, dented blue Ford Taurus stood in the road, engine running and passenger door open. I could see a driver in the car, an older black male.

LaReesa screamed, "I ain't getting in the fuckin' car wit you! Go away!"

Then Amara. "I'm yo mom! Get in the car! I ain't playin' wit you."

Sharonda stood to the side, looking scared.

I dialed 911 and told the dispatcher that someone was attempting to kidnap my daughter and please send the police, fast. I knew that was a bit of an exaggeration, but it would get them here quickly. I gave them my address and she assured me they were on their way. I rushed out to the street and stood between Amara and Reese. Amara had cut her hair and it was clipped close around her skull. She was dressed in torn jean shorts, cheap flip-flops, and a pink tank top that was a size too small.

"I need you to leave." I said, firmly.

"This ain't yo fuckin' street. I'm talkin' to *my* daughter."

"If you would like visits with your daughter, you need to contact your social worker and request visitation."

"Don't even bother, bitch! I HATE YOU!" LaReesa screamed.

I put a hand up to signal her to be quiet. "The police are on their way," I said. We could hear sirens approaching.

The man in the car had gray dreadlocks and looked to be about fifty years old. I could see two tall, silver beer cans in the cup holders of the car, between the seats. He said, "Mara, get in the car!"

Amara bowed up to me and for a second, I thought she might strike me. *Go ahead,* I thought, *let's add an assault charge to the burglary.* She stopped and listened to the sirens, then got in the car and slammed the door. They roared away down the street.

I took a picture on my phone as they sped away. LaReesa was sobbing behind me. I turned around. Sharonda had her arm around Reese's shoulders and Reese's head was bent toward the road as she cried into the crook of her arm. Sharonda said, "It's okay. She's gone. It's okay." I checked the picture to make sure I could see the license plate in it as two police SUVs screeched to a halt in front of us. The officers exited, in Kevlar vests with hands on their guns.

"She left a minute ago, but this is a picture of the car she's in."

"Which girl did she try to take? The one who's crying?"

I nodded and gestured to Reese. "This is LaReesa Jones, and the woman was Amara Jones, her biological mother. She was with a man, but I don't know who he was. She's lost custody and has not filed anything with Family Court to get visitation. She got out of prison in March, and I'm sure she is on parole, and she was drinking. Along with the driver."

The first officer walked a few paces up the street and began to speak into his radio. I caught my breath and focused on Reese. The sobs were abating and she was wiping away the tears with her hands. "Why she gotta come here? How'd she find me?"

"Did you put a return address on the letters you sent to her in prison?"

"Oh, dammit."

"It's okay. It's not your fault. We are going to stop this, though. I'm going to get something done to stop this."

The officer finished speaking on the radio and asked to talk to Reese. They stepped away and I could see him asking her questions and her answering them as he wrote down her answers. I took a deep breath, trying very hard to control my anger. *This poor kid has been through enough*, I thought, *and she needs a normal life for once.*

The officer finished his interview and said he had radioed to dispatch the license plate of the car, and said if they were drinking and driving, they'd be stopped. We thanked him for his time and the police left. I rallied the girls and we went in the house. The girls went back to Reese's room and I called Grant and told him what happened. He said he would come over later.

Grant arrived about five-thirty and we had a drink on the

back deck. The girls were watching TV in the living room. I handed him a beer as he asked, "How's LaReesa?"

"She and Sharonda were holed up in her room for the whole afternoon. Sharonda's being very supportive through all this, but she looked scared to death."

"I'm sure. What happens next?"

"I'm going to talk to Reese's social worker tomorrow and we will figure something out. Did you get your house back in order?"

"It wasn't too bad. They just opened all the closets and the cabinets. I had my only gun on me, so they didn't find one. I gave it to Detective Jefferson at the station, for the ballistics tests."

"See? You are cooperating. They can't for a second believe you had anything to do with this."

"I'm clinging to that hope."

Grant stayed for dinner and then spent the night. The girls stayed up most of the night watching videos, and all of us slept late Sunday. Grant reminded us at breakfast that he had to go furniture shopping. Cheryl texted that she was going to church and would pick up Sharonda afterward. After Sharonda was gone, the three of us headed to the block of furniture stores in downtown Hoover.

"What's your budget?" I asked.

"Negotiable. I just want to find something I like."

Grant's taste tended toward black and white, and brown leather. He asked my opinion, and I said they were nice, but leaned really masculine.

He asked, "Okay, then, if this were your house, what would you pick?"

"It's not my house."

"You're avoiding the question."

"Leather is nice, and super durable. But I'd go with more of a wine color." I pointed to an example.

"Recliner or no?"

"That's up to you."

In the end, he chose a traditional-style sofa in the burgundy color and two matching leather chairs that reclined. He paid for it all and they said they would deliver it in a month. We found Reese asleep in a recliner when we were finished, and we woke her up so we could leave. Grant showed her what he had picked out and then offered to take us both out to dinner to thank us for our help.

"Unless you are too sleepy?" he asked Reese.

"No, no. I'm fine. Never too sleepy for a burger."

We drove down Highway 150 and chose Beef O'Brady's for dinner. Their burgers were huge, and we laughed at Reese as she tried to fit a bite of the whole thing in her mouth. Somehow, she managed, and afterward Grant dropped us off, but checked the house to make sure we were safe before heading home. After he left, Reese and I relaxed in the living room.

"I'm glad y'all are back together," Reese said. "He a good man."

"I am too, and I agree."

"Good, 'cause he got you pickin' out furniture for his house. Wants to make it yo' house." She giggled.

"No, I— I don't think that's it."

"Sure, you go on believin' that."

Was that it? Was Grant thinking of asking me to move in? Or marry him?

"Has he said anything to you?" I asked.

"Not yet. But I bet it's comin'" She went down the hall to her bedroom, humming "Here Comes the Bride."

It took several deep breaths to get my anxiety under control.

Monday morning, I dropped Reese off at Dad's and went to work. I put my stuff away at my desk and asked Jessica if I could have a meeting with Mac in ten minutes. She checked his schedule and buzzed him. He agreed, although he said he didn't have much time. Then I went upstairs to the third floor. The third floor held the Foster Care Unit, overseen by my friend Danessa. I waved to her as I walked past her office. I entered the cubicles in the center of the floor and made to way to Tori's.

Tori O'Leary was my social worker. I had protested, upon hearing from Mac that Reese and I were getting a worker in the Foster Care Unit. He had reminded me, quite forcefully, that we were breaking enough rules as it was since Reese was living with me, and Tori was going to work with me, like it or not. I had no issues with Tori; she was a good worker who had started out in the Investigation Unit with me, but transferred to the Foster Care side of things as soon as she could. Many workers did. The hours were better and the work less chaotic and crisis-oriented.

Tori was at her desk, her pretty, long red hair tucked behind her ear as she focused on a form in front of her. I knocked on the wall of her office and she gestured to a chair by her desk. I collapsed into it with a big sigh.

"Uh oh," she said. "What's up?" I could barely hear a faint trace of her original Irish accent.

"Can you come meet with me and Mac?"

"Is my girl blowing her placement?" Worry etched her freckled face.

"Not at all! I just don't want to have to go through it twice. Please?"

She followed me down the one flight of stairs and Jessica told us to go in. We sat in the two chairs in front of Mac's desk. His unlit cigar was in his mouth this time, but he put it down and asked, "What's going on?"

I told them both the story of this weekend, about Amara showing up and trying to get LaReesa in the car, that she was drinking, and about calling the police and her running. I told them both how she had broken into my home before, and about Reese's missing clothes. I wanted to go to Family Court and get a no-contact order, but they both disagreed.

"We aren't there yet, Claire." Tori said. "We need to have an IM and she if she is willing to work to get custody back." An IM was an Intervention Meeting, and it guided everything about our care of children, including setting goals and planning for the future.

"She won't show up. She hasn't shown up to hearings or anything before. And Reese is adamant that she doesn't want to live with her. She says she'll run away, and I believe her."

Mac said, "Nevertheless, you know how this works. She has to be given every chance to change before we go further."

I sat back in my chair and let out a big, frustrated sigh. I'd seen this before in so many cases. Felt the resentment of the kids and their guardians as the parents promised, and failed, and promised again. But this time it was personal, and it hurt.

Tori said, "By the way, if we should get to the point where Amara's rights are terminated, would you be willing to adopt Reese?"

"Absolutely. One hundred percent."

"Well, that's good to hear. Let me go schedule an IM for next week and I'll let you know the time. I'll get a letter out this week to Amara, and we'll go from there." Tori left to go back to her office, and I stood up.

"Claire," Mac said, "I know you care about her, and we are going to do all we can to get her some stability. It takes time. You've worked here long enough to know that."

"And in the meantime, I'm just supposed to put up with this woman breaking into my home and threatening to take her?"

"Stay vigilant. Call the police if she shows up again. We will do our part and this will all work out."

I wished I shared his optimism.

Chapter Eighteen

I went back to my desk but I was finding it hard to get anything done. I couldn't get my mind to stop picturing Reese sleeping on the streets again. She'd found someone named Roderick last year when she ran away after her grandmother died who had pimped her out to other people, in return for a place to stay. She refused to let me press charges against him when she came back. She had made so much progress in the months she'd been with me. We couldn't lose it. We just couldn't.

Tori called me to ask if a week from today, Monday, July first, would work for the IM and I agreed. We set the time for three p.m. and hung up. I had to wait a week to see if Amara was even willing to come and discuss getting her daughter back. There was a better-than-average chance she wouldn't even show up, and we'd have to start this whole cycle all over again. This week was going to crawl by, and I needed to get my mind off things. I picked up my desk phone and started to schedule appointments with some clients.

My cell phone rang. The caller ID was a local number I didn't recognize, but I answered it.

"Miss Conover? It's Detective Reed Graves. I need to speak to Dylan Maynard again, and I was hoping you could help. I'm having trouble identifying this Lonnie person."

"What can I do?"

"I was hoping you would go get him and bring him to the lakeside neighborhood where his mother was found. Maybe he could point out the house he lived in, if it's there, because no one named Lonnie lives nearby that we have been able to find."

"Sure. When?"

"Today?"

"It'll take me about two hours to go get him. Let's say one o'clock?"

He gave me an address in the Eden View neighborhood where he would meet me at one and we disconnected. I called Heather and Ryan Maynard and explained, and I said I would be there about noon. I left at eleven, got gas and headed north.

Dylan was ready when I got there, clean and dressed in the Spider-man shirt and the shorts Reese had helped me pick out. On the way to Hoover, I explained why we were going there and what the police needed. We arrived at the address the Detective had given me, and a Hoover Police SUV was parked there. The engine was running so the car's interior would be cooled. Dylan and I climbed in, me in the backseat and he up front with the detective.

Detective Graves explained that this was the lake where his mom had been found and asked him if he recognized it. He nodded.

"Did you live in one of these houses, with your mom and Lonnie?"

Another nod.

"Which one?"

"On the other side," he quietly answered.

Detective Graves pulled out and drove us the five minutes or so to the other side of the lake. The houses all around the lake were large and beautiful, and all the landscaping was neat and looked professionally done. Two kids, laughing on bikes, rode past us.

"Say something when you see it, okay?" He drove slowly down the street.

"There it is."

Dylan pointed to a large, square house with tan stucco on the outside. The door was brown, and the windows trimmed in the same brown. He pointed to a window on the second floor. "That was my bedroom."

The Detective looked at me. "I've got a judge waiting to sign the warrant." He dialed a number on his phone and said they had ID'd the house. A minute later, he nodded, hung up and called someone on his radio. A few minutes after that, two more police SUVs pulled up with uniformed officers. The neighbors were starting to notice something was going on. I could see faces in a lot of the windows of the houses around us.

"You both stay right here, understand?"

We nodded, and watched as he joined the other officers and they approached the front door. One of them knocked, loudly, and called "Police!" Then they slammed the door open and entered the house. I saw Dylan wince at the noise and I reached up and put my hand on his tiny shoulder.

They weren't in there long. Detective Graves came back to the SUV and said, "The house is totally empty. He's gone."

He walked a bit down the street and got on his radio again. He talked for a few minutes and came back to us. "I think we have a last name, though. Mitchell. This house was owned by Fran Mitchell, who died last year. Londale Mitchell is her son and he inherited the property." He asked Dylan, "Does that sound familiar?"

Dylan shrugged. He was shutting down, and I could see the fear and discomfort on his face.

"You are doing a great job, Dylan." I said, as the detective walked down the street on his radio again. When he was finished, he gestured to me to join him. "I'll be right back." I walked the twenty feet or so to where Graves was standing.

"Guess what Londale was in prison for?"

"Oh, no."

"Yep. Possession of CSAM."

Great. Child Sexual Abuse Material. Terrific.

"Just Possession or actual abuse?"

"Just Possession that we know of. I've got a call in to his parole officer to hopefully get some info on where he might have gone. He's cleared this place out pretty thoroughly."

I glanced back at little Dylan. I could barely see him in the front seat of the SUV. His head was bowed, his sad face looking into his lap. Poor kid. Had Lonnie done something to him?

We heard a front door close and an older woman began walking toward us. She looked to be in her late sixties or early seventies. Her hair was dyed a golden blond which only exaggerated her wrinkled skin. She wore comfy cotton pants and a matching top with sneakers, and marched to us with a determined step.

"Good afternoon. My name is Julia Melville, and I live over there." She pointed to a house across the street, also large and lovely, with a front porch with bright-cushioned furniture that I envied. "I would like to know what is going on."

I let the detective handle this one. "Hello ma'am. We are sorry to disturb you. We are looking for the man who lives here."

"Poor Fran. That worthless son of hers moved in there after she passed away, but he moved out in the middle of the night Saturday. He had a big truck and everything. The noise was unreal. I started to call y'all, I really did. It should be illegal to make that much noise in the middle of the night. And we had a dead body in the lake last Thursday. Did you know that? I might have to put my house on the market. Did Lonnie have anything to do with that woman's death? I think it was his girlfriend. He's an evil man. Evil."

Ms. Melville stopped for breath and the detective took the opportunity. "Yes, ma'am, we are investigating the woman's death. Do you have any idea where Mr. Mitchell may have gone?"

"Oh, who knows? He's been in prison, you know. It just about killed poor his poor mother, when he got locked up. Fran and I used to have coffee together some mornings. He was always hanging around, trying to borrow money and using her computer. They confiscated it, you know, when he got arrested. Had some horrible things on it. When-"

Detective Graves broke in, "I'm terribly sorry, ma'am, but we must finish up here. Thank you for that information. We will keep the community posted as the investigation proceeds. Please call us if you see anything going on at this house." He gestured toward her house with one hand as he handed her a business card with the other.

Ms. Melville took the card, gave a small snort under her breath, and headed home. The detective looked at me and I rolled my eyes. He said, "There's no shortage of nosy folks like her here. I interviewed several of them after the body was found."

"Maybe that's a good thing."

"Sometimes nosy neighbors can be helpful. Let me give you a ride back to your car."

"Do you think Lonnie could have had something to do with Regina's death? I mean, we know based on Dylan's statement that he couldn't have pulled the trigger because they were together, but could he have hired someone? I mean, assuming Dylan's statement is true."

"At this point, anything is possible. By the way, Ms. Maynard's autopsy is happening right now. We don't expect much new information."

"Will you let me know what it reveals?"

"I will."

He took me and Dylan back to my car and we headed to Blount County. Dylan was quiet on the way up. "You doing okay?" I asked him.

"Yes."

"Was it hard to go back and see that house?"

"It makes me think of my mom. I really miss her."

"I know you do. It will get easier, with time. I lost my mom when I was thirteen. It's hard."

"Was she murdered, too?"

"No, she died of cancer."

"I'm sorry," he said so low I almost didn't hear him.

I subtly hit the Voice Memos app on my cell phone and placed it back on the console. "Dylan, listen, I need to ask you some questions. I really need you to be honest with me, and no matter what you say, you are not in trouble, okay?"

"Okay."

"I need you to tell me about Lonnie. How did you meet him?"

"He came over to our apartment, last spring. Mom said he was her new boyfriend."

"Had she had other boyfriends, before?"

"All the time. But I liked Lonnie. He played with me. He liked to play video games. He had a really cool Nintendo at his house with a big TV and we used to play all the time. We both like Mario Kart."

"What else would you do together?"

"Lots of stuff. Play baseball and soccer in the yard. But he said we had to keep our friendship a secret."

"I see. Did you have to keep any other secrets?"

Dylan squirmed and looked uncomfortable.

I said, "Remember I said that the truth was important? That it may help us figure out what happened to your mom?"

"He liked to take pictures of me. He told me not to tell mom."

"Did you have your clothes on, in these pictures?"

"Sometimes."

"Sometimes?"

"Sometimes just my underwear," he whispered. "Sometimes he made me take them off. He said it wasn't hurting anybody and it would help him get money for more video games."

"Thank you so much for telling me that. That is very helpful. Do you have video games at your new house?"

"Grandma only has one TV, in her bedroom, and it's pretty small. She doesn't have a gaming system. She and Grandpa are going to sell that camper and get me a TV."

"Well, that's nice. I bet you are looking forward to that."

He shrugged. "They don't have cable, so I won't have Nickelodeon."

I didn't know what to say to that. I turned off the Voice Memo feature on my phone.

Some time later, I turned into the long drive of his grandparents' house and the size difference between it and Lonnie's house by the lake was glaring. I told Heather that Dylan had been extra helpful, and he went to his room. Once alone with Heather, I asked how things were going, and if they needed anything.

"Thanks so much for the help with his clothes."

"Do you need me to get some more?"

"We're waitin' for Ryan to get paid. Sometimes— sometimes it takes a while. Then I'll be able to get groceries and some more clothes for him."

"Do you get any help? Food stamps, or anything?"

She looked down, an overall look of shame on her face as it slowly reddened. "Ryan says we don't need no welfare."

"I appreciate his pride, but you have a kid to raise now. They can be expensive."

She nodded. "And Dylan wants a Nintendo and a TV. There's no way we can afford that."

"Look, I hate to tell you this, but Dylan told me some things about Regina's boyfriend today that I need to further investigate. I'm going to get him an appointment at an agency in Birmingham to help me. I'll take him when it's time."

"Was he sexually abused?"

"I'm not sure. There were some inappropriate photos taken of him, and I'm not sure what else happened."

"Poor kid, abused just like his mom."

Chapter Nineteen

Oh, no. "What do you mean?" I asked, dreading the answer.

"My daddy, he touched Regina when she were a toddler. Thank God she told me immediately and I stopped it. We moved out of here until both my parents died, and I kep' her away from him."

"And you, did he--?"

"No, my sister was the one he liked."

"I'm so sorry."

She shrugged. "It happens. It happens all the time, really."

Yes, it did. I couldn't even count the number of multi-generational sexual abuse cases I had seen throughout the years. It also explained so much about Regina's behavior, including her early sexual activity, her seduction of her science teacher, and her multiple sexual partners. I offered again to help Heather if she decided to apply for any assistance, and said goodbye to her and headed back to the office. I had to get on the phone and get Dylan some services, ASAP.

Back at the office, I updated Mac then called The Cole Center. The receptionist, Kathy, and I knew each other and we chatted for a while before she gave Dylan an appointment for Wednesday at two. It was the Center's policy to not gather any information about the kid they are seeing ahead of time, so they could do an unbiased assessment. I called Heather and let her know I'd pick up Dylan at one, then blocked the time off on my calendar.

Detective Graves called late in the afternoon to let me know that the autopsy on Regina Maynard had been completed, and nothing had been found that was surprising. She'd died of multiple gunshot wounds to her chest and abdomen from .22 caliber bullets. He spared me further details, and said the Maynards had her body sent to a funeral home near them. I wondered if they'd called the county about getting some help.

Right after that, my office phone rang again. This time the caller ID said Blount County so I picked it up.

"Miss Conover?"

"Yes?" Whoever was on the line did not sound happy.

"This is Dr. Grace Allen, from Blount County High School. What the hell did you tell the police?"

"I'm sorry?"

"They've been here today, asking all sorts of questions about Regina Maynard and David Almogordo. So thanks for that. My Superintendent is now involved and Mr. Almogordo will lose his job. And I have four weeks to find a new science teacher."

I thought back. What the hell had I told the police? That's right. I told Detective Graves that she had an affair with her teacher.

"I'm sorry, Dr. Allen, but a woman has been murdered. They need to know about her past, the good and the bad. And I would think that if you have a teacher who is behaving that way with your students, that you do need to let him go."

"This is *my* school and *I* will decide who needs to be let go."

"No doubt. But--"

"And I'd appreciate it if you stay the hell out of my business!" She yelled, and slammed the phone down so the loud click rang in my ear. Russell turned around in his chair.

"Whew," he said. "Somebody is pissed at you."

"What else is new?" I muttered.

"Wanna talk about it?"

"That was Dr. Allen, the Principal of Blount County High School. Regina's school. I told the police she had an affair with her science teacher, and now she's mad at me because she has to let him go."

"Whoa. She knew about the sex and hasn't fired him?"

"Nobody has ever said it out loud before. She didn't have, and maybe still hasn't, any evidence against him. Not directly."

"And now he might sue the school system?"

"I have no idea! I've never met the man!" I snapped.

"Okay, okay. I'm sorry."

"Sorry, not your fault."

"Not your fault either, you know."

I rubbed my forehead, trying to dissuade the stress headache I could feel coming on. "I know. Christ, what a mess. I need to talk to this David Almogordo guy."

"Or you could refer it to Blount County."

"I want to get a handle on what happened before I do that. I'm not even sure we have a case. I don't have a victim, you know? She's dead. Dr. Allen and the authorities in Blount County are supposed to be investigating, but I don't really trust that is happening."

The stress headache showed up and stayed with me all afternoon. I got home Monday evening after picking up LaReesa and laid on the couch with a warm compress on my head.

"What wit you?" Reese asked.

"It was just another long day."

A knock on the front door startled us both and Reese looked out the window before announcing with a smile, "It's Grant."

She invited him in and he took one look at me and asked what was wrong. "I have a headache. And I need to find someone and I don't know how."

"What do you mean, find someone?"

"I need to interview someone, and I can't ask my office to find him because it isn't an official investigation, yet."

"Can't you just Google him?"

"You think that would really work?"

"You'd be surprised what is out there." He launched into a long story about a group of people who were able to find some celebrity due to a placement of a flag on his property. He really geeked out over the story so I tried to listen patiently, but, in the end, I said I was going to just go Google the guy. I didn't need all the flag info, but I didn't say that.

Grant followed me back to my office and I sat in front of my laptop and pulled up Firefox. I entered "David Almogordo" and waited.

For about a second. A site named "Searchpeoplefree" was listed and I could see his address in Cleveland, Alabama without even clicking on the site.

But I did click on the site, and then was shown his home

address, phone number, email address, age, and marital status. Next to all the information was a picture of his house from Maps.

"Wow. Just…wow. That was so easy."

"Yep. We live in the digital age, and it's very hard to keep stuff off the internet. It's especially bad if you use social media."

I had heard his anti-social media lectures before. He was appalled I had a Facebook page, even though I never posted anything on it, and I didn't want to hear it again. "Thanks for your help," I said, reaching for a small notebook on the desk and writing down David's address and number. "Did you need something?"

"I just came over to see if you wanted to go get something to eat."

"I'm sorry, I have such a bad headache and I really just want to go to bed and sleep."

"I'll go!" Reese yelled from the other room.

I said, "All those times she says she can't hear me when I call her. Her hearing seems fine now."

Grant laughed. "I'll take her out and get her something to eat."

"I'm going to bed."

"Do you want anything? I can bring you something back."

"No, really, thanks, but I'm going to bed."

They left in Grant's van and I took a moment to enjoy the silence. I logged on to my schedule at work and blocked off tomorrow morning, writing in that I had an appointment. I was supposed to put the name of the client and the location, but I'd worked there so long, Mac never checked up on me.

I fell into a deep sleep, only waking for a moment when Grant kissed my cheek after dropping Reese off. I woke up Tuesday morning after thirteen hours of sleep and felt so much better. I showered and was making myself some coffee when LaReesa joined me in the kitchen.

"How was dinner?" I asked.

"Good, we jus' went to the Bluff Park Diner. I had fried chicken and mashed potatoes. It was good."

"They have good food."

"He was asking me all sorta questions."

"Like what?"

"Like how I'd feel if we all lived together again. How I'd feel if you and him got married."

That shocked me for a minute. "What did you say?"

"I told him I'd be thrilled, but I want the bedroom in the basement in his house, with the private bathroom."

I laughed. "Dang, girl, you got us moved in already."

"If he ask you, you gonna say yes?"

"That is a complicated question."

"No, it ain't. If you love him, it a yes."

"But there are—"

"Stop overthinkin'. Jus' say yes and let yoself be happy."

Wise advice from a thirteen-year-old, I thought.

Chapter Twenty

I got ready for work and dropped Reese off at Dad's. I had no doubt that my relationship status would be discussed all day.

I left for Blount County, checking Google Maps along the way. David Almogordo's address was in the small town of Cleveland. It was a small craftsman-style home surrounded by lush fields of cotton that were in the process of being harvested. I parked in his driveway and made my way to the door.

I rang the doorbell, checking the time on my watch as I did. It was nine-fifteen. I wondered if he'd be home, or if he had some kind of summer employment. I lot of the teachers I knew did, just to make ends meet.

The man who answered the door was in his thirties, and my first thought was *holy cow, he is unbelievably handsome.* It seemed he had just gotten out of the shower. He could have been a model for the pair of long, red cotton shorts that tied with a string at his waist. A white towel was draped around his neck. His trim body was fit and muscular. He had caramel-colored skin and deep brown eyes below a messy mass of black hair.

"Can I help you?" he asked.

"Mr. David Almogordo? I'm Claire Conover, from DHS in Jefferson County."

"Come in?"

I entered the house into a small room with dark hardwood floors and nice furniture in dark gray, with a light gray paint on the walls. He gestured to the couch and I sat and asked, "You are a teacher at Blount County High School, correct?"

"It would be more accurate to say I was," his voice dripped in irony. "I lost my job this morning, and I think you know why. You told the police in Jefferson County that I slept with a student."

"That student was murdered, and they needed to know about her past. So you did sleep with her?"

"Regina seduced me. She was beautiful, in high school. Very sensual. She came over here one night and it happened

131

before I could even think about it."

My mind flashed back to my evening with Kirk, six months ago. I shook my head to clear it. "I understand how that can happen."

"But now I've been fired. Gracie is trying to keep me off the sex offender's list, and out of the media."

"Gracie?"

"Sorry, I've worked for Dr. Allen for nine years, it's just a little nickname I have for her. It's nothing. I'm hoping I can find a new job in teaching, but I won't if I'm fighting these allegations. And if I have to register as a sex offender, I'll have to leave teaching all together." His hands tightened on the ends of the towel around his neck, and his head bent in sorrow. His features were so dark, I thought, I doubted he could be Dylan's father.

"You are aware Regina Maynard had a baby, at age seventeen? Do you think you could be—"

"No, believe me, I did the math when her pregnancy started to show. She seduced me in January of her junior year, and her baby was born in January of her senior year. I couldn't be the father."

"And it was just the once? That you slept with her?"

"Yes! I was horrified when it happened. I ended all contact with her outside of class, and always made sure someone else was around if I had to speak to her, even in school."

"Well, with Regina dead, there is no victim. If you can keep this out of the court of public opinion, do you think you might have a chance at getting your job back?"

"I doubt it. The Superintendent is involved now. It doesn't seem to matter that it only happened once, or that it was seven years ago. I'm out."

"Do you have any idea who her baby's father might be? DHS needs to find his father."

"She dated Jerry Cook for a while that year, but there were rumors that she was quite sexually active, with many people. I can say she did seem, er, experienced."

"Do you know with whom? Any other teachers, maybe?"

"All I know is that she had a fling with one of the other

football players. Jerry Cook told me about that. He was very upset about it at the time. It hurts to be cheated on."

The guilt about what I done to Grant hit me in the chest again, full force. I took a deep breath. "Thank you so much for speaking with me. I'm sorry this is crashing down around you. It seems Regina had the power to destroy a lot of lives, and one of them made her pay."

He stood up and walked me to the door. "She probably got what she deserved."

I drove back to Birmingham and to the office. My meeting with Mr. Almogordo hadn't told me anything I didn't already know, except that he couldn't be the father, according to his testimony about when and how often his fling with Regina had happened. There was always the possibility he was lying, either about when it happened or how long it went on. With Regina gone, I doubted I'd ever know the truth.

I checked in with Jessica, who handed me a new case with her usual smarmy smile. I went back to my cubicle and reviewed it. Russ was out somewhere and I used the time to try to focus. The reporter in my new case was a female who alleged that her ex-boyfriend had molested her daughter. Not a real uncommon scenario, unfortunately. Ex-girlfriends were notorious for reporting ex-boyfriends, whether the molestation actually happened or not. I knew that for every boyfriend a single mother has, the chance that one or more of her kids would be molested increased by about thirty percent. My mind wandered back to Regina and Dylan. Was Lonnie the only one who had photographed him? Abused him? She had so many boyfriends; Dylan had confirmed that. I was anxious to see what the interview at the Cole Center tomorrow would show.

Russell entered the cubicle a short time later, grabbing a tissue from the box on his desk to mop the perspiration from his forehead. "Christ, it is hot, and it's about to storm."

"Sometimes I think you could set a clock by afternoon thunderstorms in the summer in Alabama."

My phone rang, and I reached and answered it. "Miss Conover? It's Heather Maynard."

"Hi Heather, how are you? How is Dylan?"

"He's fine. Ryan got paid and I bought him some more clothes. We got food, too, so we are okay."

"Good to hear. What can I do for you?"

"I wanted to let you and Mr. Russell know that Regina's funeral will be on Friday, at the Brayton Funeral Home up here in Hayden. The pastor from the church down the road is gonna come do it. It's at one."

"Did you call the County about getting some help to pay for it?"

"Ryan tol' his boss, Mr. Armstrong, that we was having trouble figurin' out how to pay for everythin', and Mr. Armstrong called the Home and got her cremated for us. Paid for it all."

"That's very kind of him."

"Ryan has worked for him for some twenty years. Even when things was lean."

"Well, I'm glad you got some help, and I'll see you Friday."

"Can I ask you one more thing?"

"Sure."

"I found me a black dress at the thrift store, and Ryan has a dark suit, but lil' Dylan ain't got no clothes for wearin' to a funeral. Do you know where I can get some help with that?"

"I'll tell you what. I have to pick him up tomorrow for his appointment, and I'll take him afterward and get him some dress pants, and a shirt and a tie."

"Thank you so much. I mean, it's his mamma's service, and I want him to look right."

"I understand, and I'll see you tomorrow."

I drove to Blount County the next afternoon and picked Dylan up at one. I didn't explain too much about where we were going, leaving that to the therapist. The Cole Center was on the west side of town, not far from Family Court. Kathy greeted us as we walked in the door. As usual, the office felt quiet and small.

Dylan waited patiently with me until Jay Cole joined us in the waiting room. I'd worked with Jay for years and was happy he was going to be the one to do Dylan's assessment. Jay was in his forties, a little pudgy, with his dark hair graying around the sides. He always displayed the calmest demeanor and was excellent with the kids. He nodded to me as I filled out paperwork before he invited Dylan back to his office.

I finished the paperwork and waited for them to return. An hour and a half passed, and eventually Jay walked out to the lobby and asked me back to his office. His office was a playroom, like our assessment room at work, with a desk and two chairs tucked into a corner. The desk was covered in files, much like mine. Dylan sat next to me in the chairs while Jay sat in his desk chair. Dylan fiddled with something while Jay talked, and I could see it was a star-shaped, foam stress reliever.

"Okay," he began, "Dylan and I had a good visit, and he has given me permission to tell you a few things we discussed." Dylan nodded beside me.

"Thank you, Dylan," I said.

"He has the right to stop me at any time, or add to or correct anything I say, right, Dylan?"

Dylan gave a small nod.

"He understands that this is to help him process what happened, right?" Jay asked.

Another small nod.

"We talked a lot about Lonnie, and the time spent with him. He and Lonnie liked to play video games together, but sometimes Lonnie would take pictures of him, and sometimes those were naked pictures and were uncomfortable." Dylan nodded again.

"We talked a lot about our bodies and what the parts are called, and Dylan says no one has touched his penis or his buttocks or put anything in his mouth, in a sexual way."

I breathed a small sigh of relief and Dylan asked if he could go draw at the table. Jay said he could, and he went across the room and began to color. Jay looked at me. "I do think he was extensively groomed. Promised video games for the pictures, and God only knows where those ended up. He says Lonnie has disappeared?"

"Left his house in the middle of the night."

"I hope they catch him."

"Me, too."

"I tell you what Dylan does need, though, is some grief counseling. He is having a hard time with the death of his mom."

"Not surprising."

"Do you need me to get you some names?"

"His grandmother has requested someone in Blount County. They don't have the best transportation." I could see Dylan listening to us, but trying not to look interested.

"I'll get you some names."

"Thanks so much. I have to take him to get some clothes for his mom's funeral on Friday."

Jay nodded. "We talked a lot about the blood. Let me know if you have any questions, and look for my mail."

"Thanks so much."

I gathered Dylan and we headed to Fultondale, a town north of Birmingham on the way to Dylan's house. There was a Target there and I hoped they would have what we needed. Dylan followed me around the children's section of the store as I gathered a short-sleeved white dress shirt, black pants and a pre-tied black tie that was very handy. He tried everything on in the dressing room, and after a couple of false starts, we found things that fit and I paid for them. Dylan was very quiet, and didn't request anything other than the items I purchased for him. I wondered what the visit to the Cole Center had triggered.

Once in the car, I asked, "Hey, you okay? You are a little quiet."

He squeezed the stress star again. "I'm alright. Mr. Jay gave me this to help with my anxiety." He held the foam star up so I could see it.

"Did talking to Mr. Jay upset you?"

"A little. We talked a lot about my mom and Lonnie."

I waited, wondering if he wanted to talk about anything else.

"Mr. Jay said those pictures were in—inappropriate."

"Do you know what that means?"

He nodded. "It means wrong. I shoulda told Mom."

"I'm sorry that Lonnie did that to you."

"Do you think he killed my mom?"

"I don't know. Do you?"

Chapter Twenty-One

"He said he loved us. He wanted to get money for us and for us to be happy. I was just trying to help."

I could hear the heartbreak in his voice. "I know. And you didn't do anything wrong. You know that, I hope. An adult asked you to do something so you did it, just like you are supposed to do. Please don't think any of this is your fault."

"What's going to happen to Lonnie, if they find him?"

"I imagine he will have to go back to jail for a while. Taking inappropriate pictures of kids is wrong."

"I wish none of this happened, and Mom was still alive and everything was the way it was before."

"I know. Mr. Jay and I are going to find someone for you to talk to about all this, and that will help."

He was quiet again, all the way to his grandparents' house. I walked him to the door and handed the shirt and pants and tie to Heather. "Thank you so much. I don' know how I'll pay you back."

"You don't have to. Please don't worry about it."

"You'll be there Friday?"

"I will. I'm not sure about Russell, but I'll be there."

I spent all day Thursday investigating the new case Mac had assigned me on Tuesday. At the end of the day, I referred the girl for further evaluation and headed home. I doubted she had been molested, but my doubts wouldn't close this case. Thursday evening, I went through my closet, searching for something black or at least dark to wear to Regina's funeral tomorrow.

LaReesa walked into my bedroom as I was throwing stacks of clothes on the bed and feeling frustrated.

"Whatcha doin'?" she asked.

"Looking for something to wear to a funeral tomorrow."

"Who died?"

"Remember Dylan? It's his mom's funeral."

"That bitch that accused Grant? Why you wanna go and respect her?"

"Language."

"Sorry."

"I'm going to support Dylan and his grandparents."

"Oh."

I held up a navy-blue suit and Reese exclaimed, "No! No way."

"What's wrong with it?"

"How long you had it?"

I thought back. It was so old I couldn't remember. "I don't know. Ten years?"

She gave me a look. "Don't you never go shopping?"

I sighed. "I'm always too busy." I held up a black dress that had a subtle pattern on it. "This?"

"That's, like, a cocktail dress, right? Maybe not good for a funeral?"

I agreed. I tossed the blue suit in a giveaway pile and hung the cocktail dress back up in the closet. I pulled out a black skirt and a short-sleeved top that matched, looking at Reese for comment.

"Much better."

She helped me pick out a pair of black shoes from my limited stock and said we should go shopping together. I smiled, knowing who would come out ahead in that adventure.

"So is Grant going with you tomorrow?"

"I don't know." I pulled my phone out of my pocket and called him.

"Hey. Are you going to Regina's funeral tomorrow?"

"Are you?"

"I am."

"Can I go?" Reese asked.

"Do you want to ride together?" I asked Grant.

"I can pick you up at noon. Is Reese going?"

"She wants to. She can go if she can be ready."

I informed Mac in the morning that I was going to take a personal day. I didn't have any appointments in the morning and didn't see the point in going in for just three hours. Grant arrived at eleven thirty, looking tall and gorgeous in a black suit and a black tie that had small blue dots on it. He looked amazing, and both Reese and I told him so. Reese also looked

140

cute in a black-and-white dress with tights.

We got to Brayton Funeral Home at about twelve-forty-five. We walked into the lobby and were greeted by Heather and Ryan and Dylan, who were standing by the door. Dylan had been given a haircut and was wearing his new outfit, with the tie.

"Little Man! Lookit you! You stylin'!" Reese exclaimed as she gave him fist bump. That earned her a smile.

We shook hands with Heather and Ryan who thanked us for coming. I introduced Grant as Regina's former boss. The Maynards didn't seem to realize that Grant had fired their daughter, and were very nice to him. We milled around the lobby before the service was scheduled to begin. I picked up some printed programs after I signed the guest book and handed one each to Grant and Reese.

I spotted Jerry Cook and nodded to him from across the room. On his arm was a lovely young lady about his age, who I assumed was the girlfriend he had mentioned when we met at DHS. He and Ryan were talking to a man in his fifties, with gray hair, and in a gray suit. The man was of average build, but fit, and had the demeanor and confidence of a successful businessman. I suspected he was Mr. Armstrong, the owner of Armstrong Farms, where Ryan worked.

Henrietta and Fred Maple entered and spoke with the family for a few minutes. Henrietta wore a church dress, and held Fred's arm, and he looked nice in a brown suit and tie. Different from the greasy t-shirt and apron, for sure. *Another surprise*, I thought. Just about everybody in this room had their lives negatively affected by Regina, yet here they all were.

David Almogordo walked in with Dr. Grace Allen. I suppressed the urge to hide behind Grant as she spotted me across the room and shot me a dirty look. She didn't otherwise acknowledge my presence, and neither did Mr. Almogordo. They greeted Heather and Ryan and little Dylan and went into the chapel immediately. I wondered if Heather knew about the encounter between her daughter and her teacher. I doubted it.

The Maynards greeted a few other people whom I didn't know. I looked around for anyone who met Lonnie Mitchell's description, but I didn't see anyone who I thought could be him. Dylan looked sad and his gaze was mostly locked on his black sneakers. Ryan stood behind him, one strong hand on his shoulder. Russ had texted me that morning that he had appointments and wouldn't be there.

A staff member of the funeral home announced that the service was about to begin and urged us into the chapel. Grant, Reese, and I found seats in an oak pew upholstered in mauve, near the back. Soft music played from speakers installed in the ceiling. Dylan and the Maynards sat in the front pew, on the right. Heather looked lovely in a slightly faded, cotton black dress, and occasionally dabbed at her eyes with a tissue. The door opened as everyone was getting seated, and I watched Detective Graves enter the chapel and sit alone at the back.

Regina's painted metal urn sat on a stand at the front, to the side of a wooden podium where a handsome, young brunette man in his twenties stood. He wore a black suit with a black tie and held a book, which I assumed was a Bible, in front of him that was filled with ribbon-type bookmarks. He pulled the microphone on the podium closer to him and cleared his throat. It was obvious that he was the preacher from "down the road" that Heather had found to do the funeral. I opened the program and read, Funeral Services for Regina Renee Maynard. The date was next, June 28, and the year. Officiated by the Reverend Jackson Davenport of Evergreen Baptist Church, Hayden.

Jackson Davenport. I had heard that name before, but where? I thought back. I realized with a start that he was the football player in high school that Jerry Cook alleged Regina had slept with. Well, well, I thought. One of Regina's former lovers was a preacher. My eyes scanned the room for Jerry, who was sitting a few rows ahead of us on the other side of the room with his pretty girlfriend. His gaze was locked on the Reverend, a look of pure hatred on his face.

That startled me a bit. It seemed Jerry still had feelings for Regina, if his level of anger was any indicator. His pretty girlfriend whispered something in his ear and patted his leg, then held his hand.

Reverend Davenport welcomed us all, and thanked us for

being there. He offered a prayer of thanks and blessing for the family and all who were in attendance. I bowed my head, but then raised it slightly to look around the room. Dylan and his family sat in silence, heads bowed and sad. Heather continued to wipe her tears away with a tissue. Dylan wasn't crying but he continued to stare at his feet and looked traumatized, for sure. I could see Ryan trying to be the strong one for the family, his arm around Heather as he sat straight and proud.

The Reverend moved on to talk about Regina as a person and how much she loved her son and her family. I wondered if he could be Dylan's dad. He talked about her moving to Birmingham and her attempt to make a better life for herself and her son. *Yeah, by stealing from other people*, I thought. He talked about her work in computers, and how she loved her new career. I glanced at Grant, who sat stone-faced beside me. I took his hand and held it and he gave me a small smile.

My gaze moved to David Almogordo and Dr. Allen. David had teared up a bit and wiped his eyes subtly with his hand. *Hmm*, I thought, *this is the woman, kid really, who cost you your career and now you are shedding tears for her? Interesting.* Then Dr. Allen noticed the tears and her arm went around his shoulders and began rubbing them in a comforting way. The gesture was an intimate one of support and care that made me suddenly realize she was likely more than his ex-boss.

Chapter Twenty-Two

Grace Allen saw me looking their way and immediately lowered her arm. Reverend Davenport was quoting scripture, and she bowed her head as she gave me a nervous glance, then whispered something to David Almogordo. The Reverend read John 14 as I watched Dr. Allen squirm in discomfort.

"Let not your heart be troubled; you believe in God, believe also in Me. In My Father's house are many mansions; if it were not so, I would have told you. I go to prepare a place for you. And if I go and prepare a place for you, I will come again and receive you to Myself; that where I am, there you may be also. And where I go you know, and the way you know."

Reverend Davenport assured the family that Regina's soul was at rest in the arms of Jesus as I watched Jerry Cook nod in agreement. I looked slowly behind me and saw Detective Graves, who appeared to be taking notes. A young woman got up and sang a hymn to recorded music, followed by more scripture. The Reverend stated that Regina's ashes would be interred in a private ceremony, later, and I wondered if that was for financial reasons. I doubted Heather and Ryan could afford a plot in a cemetery now. The Reverend then invited us to his church for a reception.

Grant and Reese and I made our way back to Grant's van. He typed the address of the church into his GPS in his phone as we waited to get out of the parking lot.

"Dang, that was so sad," Reese stated.

"Funerals usually are," I answered. "Do you regret missing your grandmother's?"

LaReesa had run away before her grandmother's funeral last year. "Naw," she answered. "I wouldn'a had nothing nice to say about her, anyway. My granddaddy's was sad, though."

We rode in silence to the church a few miles away. A squat, red brick building with a large white steeple sat back from the road, and the parking lot was already filling with cars. A door was open in the building attached to the church, so the three of us went there. A room was set up with bar-height tables around the perimeter, and a long table in the middle of the room held trays of cookies and fruit and cheese along with flowers. A few ladies I assumed were from the church were filling glasses with iced tea and water at a side station. Reese retrieved a few cookies and a glass of tea and met us at one of the tables.

"These cookies are good." LaReesa commented and Grant reached over and took one from her plate, broke it in half, and handed half to me. I put it back on the plate as I noticed the Reverend talking to a group of people over by the windows. He ended the conversation and went to the drinks table, where he retrieved a glass of tea and stood by himself near the table.

I excused myself from Grant and Reese and approached him. "Reverend Davenport? Lovely service."

He held out his hand and I shook it. He said, "Thank you for coming. Were you a close friend of Regina's?"

"No, my boyfriend was her last boss, at High Tech."

"Oh, yes. Grant, right? She mentioned him to me."

"You knew Regina in high school, correct?"

"Yes, we were in the same class. But she dropped out our senior year."

"Because she had Dylan."

"Yes, I believe so."

"You and Regina dated, right?"

He looked around the room, nodding to a few people. He looked uncomfortable. "Well, it wasn't anything serious," he said to me.

"It's my understanding she cheated on Jerry Cook with you. Is there a chance you could be Dylan's father?"

Suddenly the Reverend looked *very* uncomfortable. He brushed past me to the kitchen, just across the room, and motioned for me to follow him. I did, into the industrial steel kitchen. He stood in front of the large metal sink as I pushed the door nearly closed behind me.

"I really don't think this is the place to discuss this," he said, sternly.

"I would be happy to meet with you at your convenience. I work for DHS, see, and I need to find Dylan's father. He has the right to custody if he wants it."

"Please don't mention this to anyone here."

146

"What are you afraid of? Being Dylan's dad?"

A moment of silence passed. "Look, I just graduated from Seminary and this is my first job. If my history with Regina comes out..."

"So you dated a girl in high school. That's against the rules? I doubt it, or there would be no ministers. But an illegitimate child? Okay, that is a big deal, but—"

"I'm not Dylan's father. My relationship with Regina was over long before her pregnancy."

"Do you know who his father is?"

He scoffed. "Could be anyone. She was a—" He stopped himself. "She was very sexually active in high school."

I could still sense the fear and discomfort coming from him. "I don't understand what you are afraid of?"

He glanced at the door behind me as he took two steps toward me, bowing his head as if he were about to tell me a secret. Quietly he said, "We—We, um, recorded ourselves, see?"

"You and Regina?"

"Yes. We were--together--more than once. At my parents' house. We thought it would be fun, you know, to watch later. We recorded it on my phone, which she then stole. It was a brand-new iPhone. I told my parents I lost it. They were so mad."

"And?"

"And she came up here in February just after I got hired. She said she still had the recording, on her computer, and I had to pay her a thousand dollars a month if I wanted it to remain a secret. I don't have a thousand dollars a month to give her. I offered her five hundred, which was all I can afford, and that's barely. She agreed."

"She was blackmailing you."

He nodded, sadly. "If the congregation finds out, I'll lose my job, and I like it here."

"You never considered just coming clean?"

"Tell the congregation that I had unmarried sex with a girl, and it's on film, and out there somewhere? I don't think so."

"It would be easier to kill her."

A surprised look crossed his face. "Of course not! I didn't kill her. I wouldn't kill anyone! Exodus twenty thirteen makes that very clear."

"Exodus tw--?"

"Thou shalt not kill."

"Oh. Wouldn't it be lovely if those Commandments really worked?"

"It is the Word of the Lord. The Bible says—"

The kitchen door slid open and Grant appeared in the doorframe, his tall body backlit by the lights in the other room. "Hey, everything okay? You sorta disappeared."

I walked toward him and out of the door, thanking the Reverend for talking to me as I passed him on the way out.

"But you won't—you won't tell anyone, will you?" he asked.

I gave him a small smile. "Don't worry, your secret is safe. You should talk to the Detective who is investigating Regina's murder, however. Being honest with the police is the best thing you can do right now, for your own good. Detective Graves is here. He's the blond guy in the gray suit with a light blue tie."

He nodded and I went out of the door and followed Grant back to our table. Once there, he said, "Sorry if I interrupted anything."

"No, I'm glad you did. You saved me from a lecture on The Ten Commandments."

"What's the Reverend's secret he is so worried about?"

"Tell you later."

Reese had finished her cookies and we decided it was time to go. I saw the Detective on the way out and mentioned he might want to talk to the Reverend. We walked over to Heather and Ryan and Dylan, again expressing our sympathies. The gray-haired man I saw earlier was standing with them. He was indeed Mr. Armstrong, Ryan's boss, and Ryan introduced us. I told Dylan I'd see him later and we walked to Grant's van. Once inside, he asked me again about my conversation with Reverend Davenport.

"He slept with Regina, multiple times, in high school. Apparently, they recorded it just for fun and she had a copy and was blackmailing him."

"Dumb ass," LaReesa muttered.

"Indeed," I said. "Reverend Davenport is afraid he will lose his job."

I thought for a while on the way home, while Grant and Reese talked about the service. I realized Reverend Davenport had said that Regina kept a copy on her computer. But Regina didn't have a computer, at least not at her parents' house. I voiced this to Grant and Reese.

"I wonder where she kept it? If it was on Lonnie's, it's gone."

"Who Lonnie?" Reese asked.

I relayed the story of Dylan and Lonnie and Regina and the pictures. "Poor kiddo," Reese said.

"And Lonnie is currently on the run. I would imagine he's not supposed to have a computer because of his previous sentence and his parole, but that doesn't mean he doesn't. Or the police could have confiscated it, if she's had the video since high school and she saved it on one of Lonnie's computers, you know, from when he was arrested." My head was swimming with all the possibilities of where this video could be.

"Or I could have it." Grant said quietly.

Chapter Twenty-Three

"What?"

"Regina worked for me. You know I have several computers that all my staff use, and it could be on one of them. It's going to take me a while to go through it all, though."

"But you will?"

"Sure. Want me to run by the shop and grab some of them?"

"Yes, please." It made perfect sense that she would put the video on a High Tech computer, now that I thought about it. I couldn't see her putting a video of her with another man on her boyfriend's machine.

Forty-five minutes later, we pulled into the parking lot of High Tech. The shop was in a strip mall on a busy highway near the Galleria mall, next to a Starbucks. Grant had an employee in the building who was there to wait on customers, and Grant talked to him briefly as LaReesa and I watched through the big glass windows. Then, he went to the back room of the store.

He emerged a few minutes later with a stack of six laptops. They were all the same brand but of different ages and sizes. He put them in the back of the van and then we went to his house. Once at his house, he got set up at a table in the basement with the computers. He showed us how he searched the hard drives and looked for what he said was probably an .mp4 file.

We searched and waited. And waited and waited. There were lots of files saved on the computers, and it took time. After nearly an hour, on the fourth computer, Grant said, "Bingo, I think."

LaReesa and I walked over and stood behind him at his table. He pointed to a long set of files on the screen. "See? Right there." On the white screen was listed an .mp4 file called JACKSDAV.

"That looks right," I said.

Grant moved the mouse to click the cursor on it, then looked at me and then at Reese. "This may not be for young eyes," he said.

I looked at Reese. She scoffed, "You know it ain't nothin' I ain't seen or done before."

"It's okay," I said, "Go ahead and play it."

Grant clicked on the file and a video loaded on the screen. The camera faced the foot of a full-sized bed covered in a navy blue-and-green plaid comforter. A shelf full of trophies hung above the head of the bed, and the walls were a soft tan.

A young, blue-eyed Regina faced the camera as she adjusted the angle. Her hair was long and brown and straight, and she tucked it behind her ear as she finished playing with the camera. Without all the garish makeup, she was really a pretty girl.

Jackson was behind her, with his shirt off. He had a muscular body and long brown bangs that hung in his face. He wrapped his arms around her waist from behind as she said, "Hang on, it's almost ready." His arms dropped to his sides.

She turned around and faced him. His arms went around her waist again and he kissed her deeply. She stopped him, and they both turned at a better angle to the camera as she began unbuttoning her shirt in a sexy way. He kissed her again as she stood in her lacy light-blue bra and then she began to unbutton his jeans. There was a lot of kissing and moaning going on, and I was quite uncomfortable and turned away.

"What?" Reese asked me. "They both got a hot body."

"This is just, you know, very private."

"Then they should'na taped it." Reese answered.

The moaning continued as they got naked and moved to the bed. Grant also looked uncomfortable, as he said, "I hope none of my other employees have seen this. She just left it on this computer with no encryption or security or anything."

Reese shot him a look. "It's a sex tape, and it makes you think of encryption? Seriously?"

We watched, as Regina and Jackson moved from position to position to show off for the cameras. Never once did they discuss birth control, or put on a condom. At last, it was finished and Regina turned off the camera.

"I got me some new respect for that preacher!" LaReesa exclaimed. "He hot!"

"Can you imagine if his congregation saw that? They'd lock the doors behind him forever." I asked.

"Might be motive for murder, for sure." Grant said. "What should I do with it?"

"Can you copy it for me? Onto a…thing."

"A thing?" he asked, smiling. "What kind of thing?"

"You know, a thing. A portable thing." I held my fingers out in front of me, about three inches apart.

"A USB drive?"

"Yes! That's it."

Grant laughed at me as he went upstairs to get one from there. He returned a few moments later and copied the file onto it. He handed it to me and I slid it into my purse as he asked, "What's next?"

"I need to call Detective Graves and show this to him."

"I need to inspect all the computers my staff have been using, and look for other videos. We are going to have a staff meeting on Monday about appropriate use of company computers."

"Hey, how come none of the other High Tech staff were there at her funeral? They all know she is dead, right?"

"Of course. Regina didn't take the time to make friends with anyone at High Tech, and they were easily annoyed by her. Mamik especially. He thought she did nothing but take shortcuts. You know, trying to do a professional job without a degree, and not showing any interest in really learning much."

"Did you agree with him?"

"I have to admit, her work ethic wasn't stellar." His expression turned sad. "But, you know, she was a single mom and my heart went out to her. She was financially desperate when she answered my ad, and said she was willing to learn. And she was bright. That's the saddest part. She really understood the basics of computer repair, which is all I taught her. Had she come from a different background, she could have had a college degree and been quite successful."

Reese listened to Grant, a somber expression on her face. "That what it takes? A college degree? To be successful?"

Grant put his arm around her shoulders and gave her a little hug. "Not necessarily a four-year degree, but people who have some formal training in their profession do a little better, most times."

I looked at Reese, who looked a little downtrodden. "What are you thinking?"

She shrugged. "When Granny died, if I'da stayed in Midfield, I might still be hookin'. I feel like I got a chance to be successful here."

It was my turn to hug her. "Of course you do. You can be successful anywhere, hon, if you put in the work."

"But what if Amara gets me back? What if I have to go live with her again? I ain't stayin', I can tell you that." She said the last statement in a determined tone, and I could hear the fear and anger underneath it.

"We have meeting on Monday, remember? Let's worry about that if she shows up."

"She just wants to use me."

"What do you mean? Did she ever make you..." I let my voice trail off, intentionally, dreading what she was going to say next. Had she sold her? Trafficked her? I had a strong feeling LaReesa had never told me the extent of her dysfunctional relationship with her mother.

"She made me run drugs, but I've tol' you that before."

Chapter Twenty-Four

I nodded as Grant asked, "Come again?"

"I mean, you know, if her and whatever guy she was with that day needed a fix, she'd make me walk over and get it. And sometimes I delivered stuff for her dealer. Amara said the cops wouldn't think about lookin' for drugs on a kid. She made me take my backpack with my schoolbooks to put it in, and said if anybody asked, I was walkin' home from the library after doin' my homework. One time I pocketed the money and didn't get no drugs. I told her I lost it. She beat the hell outta me, but I had lunch money for like three months."

"What were you getting for her?" Grant asked.

"Whatever. Sometimes heroin. Sometimes meth. Sometimes just weed, if she didn't have much cash."

"My God," Grant said. "And how old were you?"

"Like, nine. Ten maybe. When I got to be eleven I just stopped hanging around her at the apartment. She'd want me to be there, and to do stuff with men. But I wouldn't do it. I'd find other places to be. Then she got locked up for whorin' and possession."

I let out a long sigh. "I'm so sorry, hon."

"So, like I said, I ain't gonna live with her no more, no matter what. If I have to say that to all the social workers in the world, and all the judges, I will."

"And we are going to do our best to make sure you stay with us." Grant said, and I nodded.

We spent the rest of the weekend mostly at Grant's house. His furniture would not be in for another three weeks, so he thought it would be a good idea to paint while the living room was empty. I had just recently remodeled my house and had some good suggestions about colors. In the end he chose a cheerful yellow called Jonquil, and Reese and I brought old clothes over and helped him paint.

Monday morning arrived and I reminded Reese that I would pick her up at Dad's at two-fifteen. She dressed nicely in a new dress and arranged her long braids in a pretty way. I spent the morning putting out fires for other clients and picked

155

her up as scheduled.

As she got in my Honda, I noticed she was nervous. I knew that when she was uneasy, she talked little, and in short sentences. That's the communication I got as she fastened her seat belt and we waved goodbye to Dad.

"You okay?" I asked.

"Yeah."

"You sure?"

"I don't wanna do this."

"I know, hon, but we have to see what Amara is willing to do."

She sneered, "Nothing."

"We'll see."

She was quiet for the rest of the drive to my office, and we walked together to the conference room on the third floor, where I'd spotted Grant nearly three weeks ago. I sat with Reese on the far side of the conference table, and we watched the door and waited.

Three o'clock came and went. Reese stared nervously through the glass walls and eventually asked if we could leave. "Let's give her until three-fifteen," I told her.

At three-twelve I saw Tori heading our way, a yellow folder in her arms. Amara was behind her as they approached the door to the room. Reese inhaled a long breath and I could feel her tension as they entered the room and got seated across from us.

Amara had made some effort to look nice for the meeting. Her black hair was still close-cut around her head and she had applied a bit of makeup and lipstick. She wore a loose, flowy blouse over a long skirt and many bangles on her arms. She nodded to LaReesa and me. Reese glared at her with so much hatred, I could almost feel it, like a fog in the room. I had talked to her about holding her temper before we got here, and I worried that wasn't going to happen.

Tori thanked us all for coming to the Intervention Meeting and pulled the forms out of the folder. She explained that this was a meeting to talk about LaReesa Jones's future and her visits with her mother.

Reese was trying. I could see that. I could sense her

struggling to withhold her emotions as she looked at the copies of the form Tori had handed us.

"Shall we talk about goals?" Tori asked. "It's my understanding that Amara wants to work to get custody of you back, LaReesa."

Reese didn't say anything.

"Now, in order to make that happen, Amara is going to have to do some things. She is going to need to have long-term, legal employment, and stable housing, and prove she is able to stay off drugs."

"I got a house," Amara said. "I got my parent's house, and I stay there."

Reese simmered.

"What about employment?" I asked.

"My parole officer is helping me," she said. "I got a couple of interviews next week."

"Doin' what? All you can do is 'ho." Reese scoffed. I reached over and put a hand on her arm, signaling her to settle down.

Amara took a deep breath and I could sense she was about to start screaming at Reese. Tori did, too, and quickly said, "I'm glad to hear you are working on these goals already, Amara. I am going to set you up to have random drug testing through a local agency here. You will be given a color, and you'll call a number daily, and if your color is stated—"

"Yeah, I know how that shit works," Amara said.

"Oh, good. It will be very important for you to go get tested when—"

"I know. When can LaReesa come live with me?"

"Never." LaReesa growled, low.

"Well, like I said, you'll have to pass drug tests, and get a job, and show that you are able to properly care for her."

"Ain't happening," Reese growled again.

"Now look," Amara stated, loudly. "You my daughter and you belong wit me! These white-ass women don't know what best for you."

That did it. Reese stood up, her chair sliding across the tiled floor behind her with a loud screech. She shouted, "I ain't living with you, ever! I'm doin' fine where I am! I hate you!"

Amara stood up as well, her chair making the same loud sound across the floor. "I'm yo' mamma!" she shouted. "Don't you be disrespectin' me!"

"You ain't never done nothing to git my respect, bitch! Making me git your drugs and starving me. You the worst mom EVER!"

Amara started across the table with one arm raised across her body, like she was about to backhand Reese. I stood up and pulled Reese backwards by her dress, then stood between her and the table, between her and her mother. Tori stood up and put an arm out to stop Amara. "Let's just take a break."

Reese walked around the table and left. The glass door slid shut as I watched her crash through the door to the stairs, slamming it shut behind her. My DHS colleagues in the Foster Care unit were starting to notice something was amiss and were emerging into the hallways, shooting curious looks at the conference room.

I told Tori I was going to go find Reese. I went to the stairs she had just burst through and headed downstairs. That landed me in the front lobby, where my friends Beth and Nancy worked at the front desk.

"Did you see…" I called.

"Out the front door," Beth answered.

I exited out the glass front door, quickly glancing both directions up and down the busy city street. I walked around the block to the staff parking lot, behind the building. My ancient, white Honda Civic sat in my usual parking space, and LaReesa leaned against it, crying softly.

I approached her quietly, like one might do a wild animal. I had no idea what behavior might be next. "Reese?"

"I tol' you! I tol' you I ain't gonna live with her."

"I know, and like Tori said, she is going to have to do a lot of things to get you back. So far, she has only done one thing, and that's keep the house she inherited from your grandparents. I don't think it's time to panic, yet. Let's start worrying when she gets sober."

"That ain't ever gonna happen."

"I think you are right, so we have nothing to worry about, right?" I nudged her with my elbow and put my arm around her shoulders. "Can we go back in and finish the meeting?"

"I don't want to. I don't even want to see her."

"I know. I don't either. But we have to do all these things if you want to stay with me. Amara will probably fail all these goals, and then her rights will be terminated and you can stay with me. But we have to go and set the goals so the Court can see we tried."

Reese wiped her eyes and nodded. We re-entered the building and took the elevator back to the third floor and sat again at the table. Amara had calmed down and sat quietly next to Tori. I handed Reese a tissue from the box on the table.

Tori began, "We've outlined the goals that Amara will be working on. Now let's talk about goals for LaReesa." Reese reached for her forms and we followed along as Tori instructed. "LaReesa will have to behave, stay in school and maintain good grades."

"My grades are good, and I like my school."

I nodded, adding, "She'll be in the ninth-grade next year, and she has been doing very well."

"What do think you want to do, when you get out of high school?" Tori asked.

"I'm thinkin' I wanna be a chef. Like, maybe go to culinary school. Or do hair."

"That sounds lov—"

Amara jeered, "Why you wanna be cookin' for white people? They jus' gonna keep you down like they always do."

Why can't you say one kind, encouraging thing? Just one, I thought. Reese looked like a dog who had been kicked and seemed to shrink inside herself. She didn't say anything as Tori said, "Let me just get signatures on these forms and I think that's enough for today."

She passed the original packet around and we all signed where instructed. Reese had gone very quiet and looked both sad and angry. Amara scribbled on the form and stood up. "I'll see you later, baby," she said to LaReesa. "I love you."

"I hate you," Reese said, low. The way she said it turned my blood cold.

Chapter Twenty-Five

Amara glared at LaReesa, and Tori quickly suggested they head for her car so she could drive her home. I could sense Reese's temperature starting to boil again, so I put a gentle hand on her shoulder and said, "Let's go to my office."

We went downstairs and said hello to Russell, who was working at his desk. "Hi LaReesa! How are you?" He asked cheerfully.

"Fine."

"IM go okay?" he asked me.

I shrugged. "We set some goals."

"She ain't gonna do 'em." Reese said.

"I suspect you may be right, but we have to be prepared just in case she does."

"I am not living with her."

"Message received. Not time to worry about that yet, remember?"

"I ain't gonna visit her, neither."

"Like I said, that's in the future. Let's just worry about now, okay?"

We walked to the elevator and out to my car. The humid heat was oppressive and I could see storm clouds building in the west. "We're gonna get more rain," I said.

The sky opened up as we headed south, the storm slamming my windshield with large water drops. Grant called while we were in the car and said he was done for the day and would we like to go to his house for dinner? Reese and I said that sounded good to us.

Grant asked how the meeting went once we arrived. Reese was quiet and was unwilling to say much about it. I signaled to Grant to let it go and we enjoyed a meal together before heading home. Grant kissed me goodnight and I told him I'd call him later.

Later that night, after Reese went to bed, I dialed Grant's number while in my pajamas, leaning against the pillows on my bed. He was in bed, too, he said, and then said he wished we were together. I did, too. I told him about the IM and the goals we had set."You don't really think Amara's going to do all that, do you?"

"Frankly, no. But I can't really say that to Reese, because it's not fair to her mom. And she needs to be prepared, just in case it does happen."

"She could get visitation?"

"She could, but she's going to have to be sober for a while, first. I think that's what's going to trip her up, staying clean. Hey, my cameras are still working, right?"

"Yeah, of course. Just bring up the app on your phone. Why?"

"I need to keep a close eye on Reese. She tends to act out a bit after contact with her mom. I want to make sure she is not sneaking out." I yawned a big yawn and told Grant I was going to sleep and I would talk to him tomorrow.

"Sweet dreams, my love."

"You, too, love."

The night passed peacefully, and Tuesday morning I checked in at work before heading to Atlanta to pick up my teenage boy and his sister from their grandparents. Everything had seemed to settle down a bit with his behavior and I was hopeful as I dropped them off at their mother's. Mom seemed less stressed and happy to see the kids, so I had some hope that maybe we could make this work.

My phone rang at four-thirty as I was going back to the office to do some paperwork. The caller ID read Hoover City, so I answered it. It was Detective Graves.

"Guess who the Jefferson County Sheriff's officers picked up this afternoon?"

"Please tell me it's Lonnie Mitchell."

"It is."

"What happened?"

"He was in West Jefferson County, close to the Tuscaloosa County border. He was hanging out at a playground at a park, telling parents he was a photographer who could do family and child portraits. Was showing kids his camera and everything. One of the parents got a little suspicious so she called the Sheriff's Department via 911. They showed up and, after a short chase, detained him, then ran his name, and bingo. They are transporting him here now. He had a laptop in his car, too, which also violates his parole, in addition to the violation of the no-contact-with-kids order. I'm going to interview him when he gets here about Regina Maynard, and I wanted to know if you have any questions for him."

"Can I come talk to him? I need to find out if he is Dylan's father, or if he knows who is."

"He'll be here in about thirty minutes."

"I can be there."

I called Dad on my way to Shelby County. He agreed to keep LaReesa for a couple hours extra, and feed her dinner. I told him I'd come get her as soon as I could.

I checked in at the front desk at the Hoover Municipal Center and was given a nametag and escorted to the small conference room where Detective Graves sat across from who I assumed was Lonnie. He looked rough. He had a small gash on his temple and some road rash on his cheek and forearms. He needed a shave and a haircut. His brown bangs fell over his eyes and I could see the tops of the tattoos Dylan had mentioned, on his hands and above his collar. His hands, cuffed, sat on the table in front of him.

"This is bullshit," Lonnie said as I sat next to Graves. "Who are you?"

"I'm Dylan's social worker."

"Oh. How is he?"

"Traumatized, really, over the death of his mom."

"Sorry to hear that. He's a good kid."

"He is indeed."

Detective Graves asked, "Do you know who killed his mom?"

"It wasn't me."

"Do you know who may have had conflict with her? Anyone she had a beef with?"

"Nah, she never mentioned no one."

"Are you Dylan's dad?" I asked.

"No! I didn't meet Regina until last February."

"Did she ever mention who his dad might be?"

"She tol' me she didn't know. She had slept with a few

163

men around that time and it could be any one of them. She liked sex for sure." He said the last statement with a lick of his lips and a smarmy smile to Detective Graves.

"Did she ever mention any names?"

"No."

"Would you be willing to take a paternity test, to prove you're not his father?" I asked.

"Whatever."

I glanced at the Detective, out of questions. Lonnie said, "Will you tell Dylan I said hello?"

"What did you do with the photos you took of him?"

He looked a little shocked that I knew of them. "I sold those to a private collector. Top dollar. He's such a cute kid."

My stomach turned a bit at that statement and I could see Detective Graves bristling. He said, "You ever mess with him? Do you like the little ones, Pervert?"

"Nah, man, that ain't my thing. Me, I like the ladies. I just provide pictures to those who like to look."

"You are a sick bastard," the Detective said.

"Hey, man, I don't traffic the kids or nothing. Like I said, I'm not into that. But I make good money, taking pictures. I'm just a photographer."

"And part of the problem," I said. "If you really care about Dylan, you should help the police find Regina's killer."

"I swear I don't know who offed her. I know she had some income that she wouldn't explain to me. All the sudden she'd have all this money, be buyin' clothes and makeup and shit. She never would tell me where she got it. Maybe she sold her son."

The detective stood up, suddenly, and knocked on the door. Two uniformed officers came into the room and hauled Lonnie out of his chair. They took him out of the door and I focused on Detective Graves.

He said, "Sorry, I can't stand that guy. Or anyone who takes advantage of kids."

"Wow, you would hate my job."

"Yeah, I would."

"Did you talk to Reverend Davenport, after the service?"

"For a minute. He said he and Regina dated in high

school."

"And?"

"And what? That's all he told me."

I sighed, and reached into my purse to get the thumb drive Grant had given me. I handed it to him.

"What's this?"

"That's what Reverend Jackson Davenport should have told you about. He and Regina made a sex tape when they were in high school, on Jackson's phone, which Regina then stole. She contacted him in February of this year and said she had it, and was blackmailing him to keep it a secret. That may explain where that extra income that Lonnie was talking about came from."

The detective rolled his eyes skyward. "I was wondering why you told me to talk to him."

"As they say, now you know."

"And the right Reverend doesn't want this known in his community, for sure. Plus, now he has motive to kill her."

"For sure. Regina had copied it onto one of the computers at High Tech, but she may have made more copies when she was fired in January, before she left."

"Add to that all the theft she did before, for years. My list of suspects is getting longer, not shorter."

"Yeah, I'd hate your job as much as you'd hate mine."

Chapter Twenty-Six

I got to Dad's at six-thirty to pick Reese up. He was making tofu and vegetables for dinner and asked us both to stay. He was stirring food on the stove, and Reese was scowling.

"I don't have to eat this shit, do I?"

"Language."

"Sorry. Stuff. I don't have to eat this stuff, do I?"

"My father has invited us to dinner, and we are going to be polite and eat it. You might like it."

"Ugh. What is it, anyway?"

"It's tofu," Dad said.

"Yeah, but what is it?"

"It's bean curd." I answered.

"What?"

Dad chimed in, "It's really coagulated soy milk. It's been eaten in Asia for two thousand years."

"Yuck." LaReesa looked at me. "Can we get a pizza?"

I laughed. "No."

Dad served the stir-fried vegetables and tofu with soy sauce and chili oil. LaReesa picked at with her fork and eventually tasted it after pushing it around her plate.

"Well?"

"Tastes okay," she said, after swallowing. "Weird texture."

I swallowed a snap pea. "It's good for you. It's high in protein."

"So's a pizza," Reesa muttered.

"How was your day?" Dad asked.

"Good, for the most part." I looked at Reese, "The police picked up the guy that took those pictures of Dylan."

"Hope they put him under the goddamn jail," Reese stated.

"Again, language."

"Jeez."

"What are you doing for the Fourth?" Dad asked.

"Oh, yeah, I have Thursday and Friday off." Thursday was the Fourth of July.

Reese shot me a look as Dad laughed. "You never remember the holidays," he said.

"As of yet, I don't have any plans. I imagine Grant and I will do something. Reese? What about you?"

"Can I have Sharonda over? And can we get some fireworks?"

"Let me talk to Grant."

"And we need to start talking about my birthday," Reese added. "I want to have a party."

"Do you now?" I laughed. "I guess your fourteenth birthday is something to celebrate, come to think of it."

"Can I?"

Reese would be fourteen on July twenty-ninth. "We have time to discuss it, and yes, we will do something to celebrate."

"Wicked!"

We helped Dad clean up after dinner and headed home. I called Grant in bed before I went to sleep, and he, like Dad, asked what we were doing for the Fourth. "Do you want to go downtown, like last year?"

Last year, Grant and I had gone on our first date on the Fourth of July. We had taken a small picnic down to the University of Alabama-Birmingham campus, and watched the fireworks launched from Vulcan Park on top of Red Mountain. It had been so much fun. I thought about all the changes in the last year, like LaReesa joining my family and my now-new relationship with Grant. I felt grateful.

"Reese wants to have Sharonda over and she's asked for fireworks," I said. Technically, they were illegal in Hoover, but everybody shot them off anyway, so long as we weren't under a fire warning. "She also wants to have a birthday party at the end of the month."

"Great! I'll get the keg!"

I laughed. "God, can you imagine?"

"She's getting older, and drinking is going to be an issue, you know. It is for most teens."

"As I said to Reese recently, let's not worry about the future. Take it as it comes."

"Speaking of the future, I really wish we were together every night. Would you consider living together again?"

I was quiet for a few moments. Then, "Yes, I'd consider it."

"What about something more permanent?"

"And legal, you mean?"

"Yes. Would you consider that?"

"Absolutely."

"What kind of rings do you like?"

I was suddenly finding it a little hard to breathe. "I like rings that are classic. Antique, maybe. And not too big or expensive."

"Very practical."

"I'm a practical girl."

"Shall we go look together? Maybe this weekend?"

"That could be fun. I need to take Reese school shopping anyway, as she keeps reminding me."

"Let's go Saturday."

"And the Fourth? Let's hang out over here? Maybe cook out? And can you get some fireworks for the girls?"

"I've got a recipe for baby-back ribs I want to try. And yes, I'll get the fireworks."

"Sounds good. Five?"

"See you then. I love you."

"I love you, too."

I finished work on Wednesday and picked LaReesa up at Dad's. They had nearly finished cleaning out all the extra stuff in his house. The basement and garage were neater than I'd seen them in years, and I praised all their hard work. Dad had plans with Vicky for the fourth but wished us a good time.

In the car on the way home, I told LaReesa that Grant would be coming over tomorrow and bringing fireworks. "Grant is going to shoot them off, and Grant only, understood?"

"Aww."

"And then Saturday we are going shopping, if you want to join us?"

"Yay! Shopping for what?"

"Well, we can get you some more school clothes, and Grant and I are going to look at rings."

"Wait, what?!" she squealed, loudly.

"We are looking at engagement rings."

"He asked you?"

"Not yet, not officially. He just wants to get an idea of what I like. How do you feel about this?"

"Are you kidding? That's the best news in the whole world! Can I be a bridesmaid? What color do you think you want for your wedding? Can it be pink? I'd love a pink dress. Or maybe blue. Black and white is really cool, too--"

"Whoa. He hasn't even asked me yet." The tightness in my chest was back. "It's not time to start planning." I suddenly realized that in the very near future, I possibly would have to find the time to work, raise a teenager and plan a wedding. Not to mention selling my house and moving. "But when he does, I'm going to need your help."

"Of course! Fun!"

"I'm glad you're excited."

"You're not?"

"I am. Just anxious."

"Relax. It's going to be fine. You love each other, right?"

"Yes."

"Then that's all that matters."

She was right.

Chapter Twenty-Seven

Thursday, Grant arrived with his arms laden with groceries. He'd bought two full slabs of ribs and all the seasoning and things to go on them. He busied himself in the kitchen. I had made potato salad in the morning, and it was chilling in the fridge.

I had also asked Sharonda's parents over to join us to eat and celebrate. They arrived at five, and I got to spend some time with Sharonda's dad, Chuck. He was very nice and we chatted as we sat outside as the ribs grilled and Grant shot bottle rockets and fountains off for the girls. The food was delicious, and both Sharonda and Grant spent the night. We all fell into bed long after midnight, exhausted from all the fun.

Friday was a lazy day hanging around my house. Sharonda went home, but Grant stayed over again. Saturday morning LaReesa was ready to go at ten in the morning and already talking about the clothes that she wanted for school. We drove in Grant's van to the Summit shopping center in the east part of town. It was a newer shopping center that sported a Trader Joe's, along with a Belk's department store and several nice restaurants. Two jewelry stores were there, too.

Grant parked outside one of the jewelry stores. LaReesa was excited, and skipped ahead of us to the door. The heaviness in my chest was back and I took some deep breaths.

"What's wrong?" Grant asked.

"Nothing. It's just anxiety."

"Do you not want to do this?"

"No, no. It's not you, I promise, or the idea of marrying you. It's just change. I don't react well at first to big changes."

He stopped and took my hand. "Are you sure? I mean, we don't have to-"

"I swear, it's just a little overwhelming, that's all. Exciting, but overwhelming. I mean, I'm assuming we are going to live in your house, so I'll need to sell mine. And work, and plan a wedding, and--"

"What was it you were saying to Reese yesterday? Let's just focus on the now."

I nodded as Reese yelled, "COME ON!" from the door to

Divine Diamonds.

The saleslady was very nice and showed us several cuts of diamonds. Grant had done his research and asked about color and clarity and the origin of the stones. They talked about polish and symmetry and fluorescence and I decided, after some time, that I liked a diamond-shaped diamond, called a Marquise cut. I liked a gold band without too much clutter or other stones on it. And a diamond that wasn't too big. Grant nodded as I made these decisions, and LaReesa was smiling broadly.

"You ready to go shopping?" I asked her.

"Yeah, of course."

We walked over to Belks and Grant and I waited patiently while Reese tried on what seemed like half a million pieces of clothing. We found some jeans that looked nice on her and a few short-sleeved tops that would appropriate for school. After we'd paid for it all, we hit the Taco Mama down the way, where I ordered a Mama's salad with grilled chicken.

"You don't want no tacos?" Reese asked.

"Not if I'm going to fit in a wedding dress," I answered.

"Speaking of weddings," Grant said, "have you thought about a location?"

"Nope. Sure haven't."

"Any thoughts?"

I thought for a minute. I had not been brought up in a church, so that wasn't an option. An outdoor wedding would be lovely, depending on the time of year. I suddenly pictured having the wedding at my dad's house, on the back deck, overlooking Jones Valley. I doubted it would be big enough to hold everyone I'd want there. Maybe Grant's house, I thought. Or there were some gardens that would be lovely. I said this out loud.

"That is an idea we could look at. A garden wedding would be nice. Not in the summer, though, it's too hot."

LaReesa grinned. "What about at Vulcan?"

Reese referred to the cast iron statue that sat atop Red Mountain and overlooked downtown Birmingham. Built by Italian sculptor Giuseppe Moretti and shown at the World's Fair in 1904, Vulcan was finally placed on top of Red

Mountain in Birmingham in 1939. Vulcan was fifty-six feet tall, a hundred and eighty feet with his pedestal, and honored the city's iron and steel history. The view of downtown from the ten-acre park was amazing and the museum had an event space that would make a lovely reception. "That's one idea," I said. "We should look at Aldridge Gardens in Hoover, too. But we are not engaged, yet." I took a deep breath as the restaurant staff called our number and Grant rose to get our food.

"But you are going to be," Reese said.

"I know, but I just need to slow down the planning right now, okay?"

"Why you so nervous?" Reese asked, as Grant returned with our tray.

"What's coming up is a lot of change. Change makes me anxious."

She grabbed a taco and said, "You gotta learn to roll with it."

"How did you learn? To roll with it?" I asked.

She swallowed her food and said, "When you ain't got no one taking care of you, you just do. It's part of takin' care of yoself."

That was a little heartbreaking from an almost fourteen-year-old. I glanced at Grant, who reached one of his long arms over and stroked her shoulder. "You got people now, you know?"

Reese smiled her gap-toothed smile. "I know. It's good, too."

The restaurant was getting crowded, full of shoppers on a Saturday. I realized we had gotten there at just the right time and that all the tables were now taken. It was loud, too, filled with couples and families and groups talking and laughing. I heard one happy giggle from a nearby table by window, and glanced over there to see who was having such a good time.

A couple sat there, across from each other, holding hands across the table. I realized, with a start, that it was David Almogordo and Dr. Grace Allen, from Blount County. They were amidst a number of shopping bags, some from Trader Joe's and some from Barnes and Noble. That made sense, I thought, since they didn't have those stores up in Blount County. I watched as David leaned across the table and kissed Dr. Allen lightly on the lips.

I stood up and excused myself from Grant and Reese, saying I'd be right back. I made my way through the crowded restaurant and stood in front of their table.

"Hi." I said.

Dr. Allen glared at me. "What are you doing here?"

"School shopping. You?"

She let go of David's hands. "We were just enjoying a day out."

"Very cozy."

"Look, David doesn't work for the school system anymore. There's nothing wrong with us seeing each other."

David looked sheepish. I responded, "I never implied there was."

"We are grown adults and we can see who we like."

"Indeed. I just wanted to say hello."

"Oh, well, hello then."

"Enjoy your day."

I rejoined Grant and Reese at our table and stabbed more pieces of cucumber. They were laughing about something, then Reese asked, "Where'd you go?"

I swallowed the piece of salad, lowered my voice and said, "That couple over there, the lovey-dovey ones? That's the teacher that Regina Maynard slept with in high school. That woman used to be his principal, before he was fired because I told the police he slept with a student."

"Dang, that dead woman got good taste. She had some hot men."

I ignored that. "They sure have done a lot of shopping if one of them is unemployed." I mused.

"The benefits of being a boy-toy, I guess." Grant said. "That's quite an age difference, too. I wonder if the principal is married? Or was married?"

Dr. Allen was in her fifties, easily. Mr. Almogordo looked to be in his thirties. I shrugged. "I don't know, and I don't care. I can't imagine their relationship has anything to do with Regina's death."

David and his "Gracie" stood up and headed for the door. She held all the bags, and David's arm went slowly around her waist and he held the door for her once they reached it.

I focused back on my table. "I think we are pretty good, as far as school clothes go, right?"

"Yeah, I just need some shoes. Can we order those online? There's a pair of sneakers I want."

I hated to think what those were going to cost me.

We had another lazy day at Grant's house on Sunday, and Reese and I went home Sunday evening. Getting up for work on Monday after four days off was going to be a struggle, and I went to bed early, leaving Reese watching a movie on the couch.

Monday was a crazy day. Russ was out for most of the day, and I spent the day tracking down resources for some of my families who needed emergency funds. There wasn't much out there and I had little success. I felt frustrated as I left for my afternoon appointments with clients at one-thirty.

My white Honda Civic was parked in its usual spot. I walked to it, saying hello to my colleague, Sydney Trimble, as I did. I opened the door and sat down, reaching into my purse for my iPhone, intent on playing some music to cheer me up. Ugh, I realized, I'd left my phone on my desk. I sighed as I got out of the car and headed back toward the entrance of the building. I was ten feet away from the door when there was a very loud bang and the sound of glass breaking behind me. I felt stabbing pain in my right shoulder and down my back, and then I fell to the ground. I could hear car alarms blaring as I blacked out.

Chapter Twenty-Eight

My eyes opened, slowly. I had no idea where I was. I was in a bed, back slightly raised, in a room with off-white walls. I could hear a machine beeping. My right shoulder felt different. I looked at it, seeing a big, clunky white bandage that covered my whole shoulder. I could feel it down to below my scapula. The shoulder was numb.

Hospital. I was in a hospital. I looked at the foot of the bed to see my father, standing next to Mac, both looking concerned. Grant towered behind them both. And there was someone else. A guy with spiky black hair and blue eyes, who wore a lilac polo shirt and gray shorts. Kirk Mahoney.

"Well, welcome back!" Kirk said.

"What are you doing here?" My mouth was dry and I could feel my lips were chapped. My throat hurt, too, and my voice was scratchy. Grant squeezed by Mac and Dad, picked up a plastic cup with a straw in it and gave me a drink of water.

"Police scanner said there was a car bomb at the DHS building in Birmingham. I knew it had to be you."

"Yeah," Mac mumbled. "What is it with you finding all this trouble?"

"I don't find trouble, it finds me. What time is it? Where's LaReesa?"

Dad said, "It's after nine at night. She's with Sharonda at the Fowler's. I'm about to go call her and update her. She's really worried."

"What happened?"

"Somebody bombed your car this afternoon," Mac said. "Sydney Trimble is still in surgery, and the doctors aren't optimistic she is going to make it."

That news hit me like a blow. Sydney was in my unit and was a relatively new hire. She was only about twenty-four years old. I put my hands over my face and breathed for a second.

The door to my room opened and a man peeked his head in, then entered when he saw me awake. "Hey," he said. "Glad to see you're alert."

"Hey, Detective," I said.

Detective Graves glared at Kirk. "We are not ready to make a statement to the press."

"I'm just here as a friend of Claire's."

Grant glared at Kirk.

"You're friends with this guy?" Detective Graves asked me, incredulous.

Mac snorted.

"It's complicated." I croaked.

"Look," Graves said, "I need to speak to Claire alone. Can we have the room, please?"

Grant asked, "Do you need anything?"

"Maybe another blanket?"

"How's your pain?"

"My shoulder is numb still. My throat hurts, though."

"They had to intubate you for the surgery. I'll get you some cough drops."

"Thanks."

He left, and Dad said, "I'll go call Reese," and followed him out, then Kirk followed him.

I took a deep breath and focused on the detective. He said, "You've got quite a crowd of people who love you."

"I am very lucky."

"You are luckier than you know. Had you had been a little closer to your car, that shrapnel would have hit your neck, or your head, and you very well may not have survived."

My mouth was dry again, and I took another sip of water. "What happened?"

"There was a pipe bomb under your car, detonated by a Remote Activation Device. The device was a walkie-talkie. Someone was watching you, and hit the button when you got in your car. Luckily, it seems to have been slower than they anticipated, or been delayed, or something, and you were able to get out of your car and get some distance from it. The bomb contained ball bearings, and that's what hit your shoulder."

"That's terrifying."

"We need to go over everything about Regina Maynard's death again, unless you suspect this could be one of your other clients? I asked Mac McAlister and he said he didn't think you had any other violent or threatening cases right now. Is he right?"

I nodded. "No other threats, recently."

"Then what's different, now?"

"My family and I went shopping Saturday at the Summit. We had lunch and ran into Dr. Grace Allen, the principal at Blount County High School, and David Almogordo, the teacher who slept with Regina. They are seeing each other. Dr. Allen said that since David no longer works for the school system, they are allowed to do that. Shouldn't we be looking for someone who knows how to build a bomb?"

"Anyone can learn to build a bomb. The instructions are on the internet. This was a pipe bomb, and not anything too difficult. Remember the bombing at the mayor's office, last January? Same type thing."

I nodded. "I was the social worker for the kid who belonged to the young man who died, and James Alsbrook killed himself in our lobby."

"I forgot about that. No wonder Mac is talking about you being in the middle of all this mess, constantly."

"Like I said, I don't find trouble, it finds me."

The door to the room opened and Grant asked, "Can I come in?"

"Sure, we are nearly done here."

"You doing okay?"

I nodded, and he handed me a warm blanket and a small bag of honey-flavored drops from the gift shop. "For your throat."

"I have to get back to work, but I'll be in touch." The detective said as he left.

Grant and I were alone. "Really, how are you feeling?"

"My shoulder is still numb, so that feels fine. The drops will help my throat. What happened? After the bomb?"

"Detective Graves called me and told me what happened, and I called Reese and your dad. You are at UAB Hospital, by the way. The doctors pulled ball bearings out of your shoulder and back. Do you feel dizzy or nauseous? The doctors are worried about a closed head injury. You were unconscious for a while."

"No, nothing like that. Just a mild headache. When did Kirk show up? I'm so sorry he's here."

"He showed up about thirty minutes ago."

"What time is it?"

He glanced at his watch. "It's nine-forty."

I looked at the window, which was dark. "At night?"

"Yes."

A nurse joined us, checking the IV which was slowly dripping a clear liquid into my left arm. "How's your pain level?" She asked.

"I'm still numb."

"That will wear off in a few hours."

"How many ball bearings did they…"

"They removed six that were fairly deeply embedded. You are so lucky that they didn't hit your neck, or your head."

Mac came into the room, looking somber. I looked at him, wondering what was wrong.

He cleared his throat. "Sydney Trimble died in surgery."

"Oh, God."

"There was just too much damage, too much blood loss. The doctors are with her parents now, and the Detective. Dr. Pope is on her way, and will talk to the press."

Poor Sydney. What the hell was going on? Two young ladies were dead, and I had no idea who tried to kill me. I could feel the tears building behind my eyes. Grant noticed and walked over and held my hand. I looked at him. "You gave Graves the list of people that Regina stole from?"

He nodded and said, "Yeah, when we first met with him, since there's a chance that one of them is a murderer. Now possibly a double murderer."

"What the hell did Regina have or know that caused her death? And now Sydney's." I wiped the tears away with my fingers.

Grant handed me a tissue and I used it to clear the tears. Grant said, "There's clearly something we are missing."

Dad came back in the room. "I talked to LaReesa. She is glad to hear that you are awake and sends her love. I'm going to go get her and she'll stay the night with me."

"Thanks, Dad. I love you."

"I love you, too." He came to my side and leaned to kiss me on the cheek. "You sleepy?"

"A little."

"Tell the nurse if you get uncomfortable. I'm sure they can give you something to help you sleep."

"I'll be okay."

Dad looked at Grant. "You headed home?"

"I think I'll stay here."

"Take good care of our girl."

"You know I will."

Kirk came back in the room a few minutes later, to say goodbye. He'd talked to Dr. Pope, he said, as well as Sydney's parents and was leaving to go back to his hotel to write and file his story.

He asked "Will you call me later? My number is still the same."

I was falling asleep. "Probably not," I muttered. Grant had found a blanket and had settled his long body in the chair next to me.

"Bye!" he said to Kirk, with a big smile.

I smiled and drifted off.

Chapter Twenty-Nine

I woke up hours later feeling much more refreshed, but the nerve block in my shoulder was wearing off and it was sore. Grant was gone. I pushed the button to call the nurse and a different one from last night responded, a male one. He came in the room, checked my shoulder, told me Grant went to get something to eat, and that he would get me some pain meds. I asked him what time it was he said eight-thirty a.m.

A detective from the Birmingham Police Department entered and interviewed me for about ten minutes. He was investigating Sydney's murder, and I told him everything I remembered, but I had no idea who had done this. I referred him to Detective Graves.

Afterward, I was alone for about five minutes when the door opened again. Reese peeked around the door and saw me awake and exclaimed, "Hi!" She rushed over to me and acted like she was about to throw her arms around me, but I stopped her.

"Wait! Please! Please don't touch me," I said. "I appreciate the thought, but I'm in a lot of pain right now."

"Yeah, sorry. You want me to get the nurse?"

"He's coming back with meds in a minute."

Dad walked in the room, slightly out of breath. "Reese was so anxious to see you she ran ahead. Left me in her dust."

"Keep up, old man." Reese said.

"LaReesa." I said, sternly.

"I'm just pickin'."

"How do you feel?" Dad asked.

"The nurse is bringing me pain meds in a second cause I'm a little sore, but other than that, I'm okay."

"You got some sleep?" Dad asked.

"Yeah, a lot. I'm well rested."

The nurse, whose name badge said Zac, walked in with an IV bag. "Here we go, you've got the good stuff." He fiddled with the IV, changing out the old bag and hanging the new. "Breakfast is on the way up." He encouraged me to call him if I needed anything and left.

"What happened to my car?" I asked Dad.

"Detective Graves said they had it towed to a lab for further tests and to gather evidence. I'm afraid it's a total loss."

I was sad to hear that. I'd driven that little car around for years now. "That doesn't surprise me, but I need to call my insurance company. What happened to my purse? I was carrying it when I went back in the building to get my phone before the bomb went off."

"I think the paramedics probably grabbed the purse when they transported you. Let's see." Dad walked over to the small closet and opened the door. I could see my pants hanging there. My shirt was gone. Once upon a time, the pants had been white, but the top part was covered in reddish-brown bloodstain now.

"God Almighty," I muttered.

Dad turned and saw the look on my face and closed the door, quickly. "Yeah, your purse is in there. You okay?"

Grant walked in, took one look at me, and said, "What's wrong? You're as white as a sheet."

"She just saw the blood on her pants," Dad said. "God, I'm so glad we didn't lose you."

I looked at Grant. "I need to call my insurance company about the car."

"I'll take care of it," he said, walking to the closet. His tall body shielded my view of the pants as he found my purse on the floor of the closet.

The door opened again and a doctor walked in. He introduced himself as my surgeon, and everyone was quiet as he examined me. He gently peeked under the bandages, and told me a nurse would change them in a bit, after the pain meds kicked in.

"I removed six ball bearings from your shoulder and back. You've got some muscle damage that's going to need some physical therapy, and your scapula is fractured. It should heal in six to ten weeks. You'll be in a sling for a while."

"When do I get out of here?"

"I'm going to wean you off IV pain meds today. Transition you to pills for the pain and antibiotics. If all goes well, I don't see why you can't go home tomorrow, so long as there're no further concussion symptoms."

That was good to hear. Dad and Reese headed home, and Mac came by at lunchtime and said he'd had Jessica the secretary cancel all my appointments for the next two weeks. He also brought me my cell phone which he had retrieved from my desk. My voice mailbox was full, it said. I spent most of the afternoon wading through messages. Many were from my clients, who heard on the news there was a bombing at DHS and wanted to know if I was okay. I made a list of people to call back, and did so.

One message was from Heather Maynard. "Hey, Miss Conover, I was wonderin' if you done got that counselin' set up for Dylan yet. He ain't doing too well. He has nightmares and wakes up screaming, and he's just really sad. Call me back when you can."

I had been waiting for the report from Jay Cole in the mail with a list of possible therapists. I called Jessica, who was less than delighted to hear from me. I asked her to check my mailbox for anything from Jay at the Cole Center. She called me back and said I had a letter from him.

I asked her to read it to me, which she did after a loud sigh of annoyance. Jay's report outlined everything we had talked about in his office, about how Dylan had been groomed and promised video games for his participation in the photos. At the end of the letter, he listed four therapists in Blount County who worked with kids with depression and grief. I started to make some more phone calls, hoping one of them was taking new clients. Grant walked in, and I got a lecture on how I needed to rest. I promised to nap as soon as I dealt with these calls.

I scored on the second phone call. Jay's letter had strongly suggested a male therapist, and there was one in Hayden who was an LPC, a licensed professional counselor. His name was Oliver Pointer and he could see Dylan this week for an intake appointment, and understood why I couldn't be there. I called Heather Maynard and told her the time and place, and told her they would charge Dylan's Medicaid. She asked me about the bombing and I told her I was doing fine and we were very sad about Sydney's death.

Royanne called to check on me, having heard about the bombing on the news. I updated her on everything that had happened with my shoulder, and then with Grant. We talked for nearly an hour.

We disconnected and Grant walked over and physically took my phone out of my hands. "Enough. Rest."

"But—"

"Rest. You are not going to heal well if you don't follow the doctor's instructions and rest."

"I don't do well, sitting still."

"That's the damn truth."

The pain meds were starting to work and I was getting sleepy. I napped for a few hours and I woke up to a nurse who said it was time for more pills. I took them and she helped me to the bathroom, which made my shoulder uncomfortable, to say the least. She settled me back in bed.

Grant came back about seven, after I had supper, and offered to stay the night again and be here tomorrow for my discharge.

"You are so sweet," I said. "Are you sure you don't need to be at home? Or at work?"

"Work is covered for now. I'm just doing some interviews and hiring for the next project, but it's nothing that can't wait."

"I can't imagine that chair is comfortable. Why don't you go home and get some sleep? I'll be fine."

"I'll be here in the morning," he said, and kissed me goodbye.

He left and I perused the shows on television, finding nothing that held my interest. I turned it off and closed my eyes. I just couldn't get my mind off the bombing. I didn't remember much about it, just sitting in my car and realizing I forgot my phone. Who would want me dead? Was it related to Regina's death? That was my first thought. Whoever had killed her wasn't afraid to kill again. But why?

She'd pissed off a lot of people. Dr. Allen, for one. Regina had taken down and blackmailed one of her favorite teachers. But now they were free to see each other, so why would her death be necessary? Revenge for ruining David

Almogordo's teaching career?

There was the Reverend Jackson Davenport, too. He was the one whose career was really threatened. If word broke of that sex tape, his preaching days in Alabama likely would be over.

Then there was Lonnie Mitchell. He was supposedly out with Dylan the afternoon that Regina was murdered. He had a history of criminal activity and had been in prison. He could have hired someone to kill Regina, but why? Had she found out about the photos of Dylan and threatened to report him to his parole officer?

And why would someone shoot Regina, but bomb my car? Why switch MO's? Not to mention all the people that Regina stole from while she was working for Grant. There were at least five that I knew of, maybe more.

My eyes opened as I had a new thought. The scariest one of all. Maybe the bombing had nothing at all to do with Regina Maynard. Maybe it had something to do with Amara Jones.

Chapter Thirty

That was ridiculous, I thought. Amara wouldn't have any knowledge about bomb making. She'd been more confrontational in her relationship with me, certainly not shy about telling me how she felt.

I finally fell asleep, and was awoken by a nurse the next day who said my discharge would be later this morning. I called Grant and updated him, and asked him to bring some clothes with him when he came to get me. He agreed and said he'd see me about ten.

The surgeon came by again and rechecked everything. He cleared me to go home and instructed rest for a few more days. He'd referred me to a home-health company who would send someone out to change my bandages. They took off the bulky ones and put on smaller ones, and fitted me with a sling that I could take home and would be in for at least the next six weeks. The surgeon would see me in a week for follow-up. The nurse came in and bathed me, and helped me dress when Grant got there with the clean clothes. I threw away the formerly white, blood-stained pants. I didn't think I could get them clean, and didn't want the reminder anyway.

Grant and I got back to my house early in the afternoon. It was good to be home. I called Dad and updated him, then he brought Reese home. Grant settled me on the couch with a blanket and plenty of pillows. LaReesa hovered around me, asking, "You okay?" every two minutes.

"Yes, Reese, I'm fine. Really."

"You want something to drink?"

"No, thanks, I'm good."

Grant came in from the kitchen. "She okay?"

"I'm fine," I answered.

"You need anything?"

My patience was waning. "Ya'll. Really. I love you both, but I'm okay."

"Text if you need somethin'" Reese said, and headed for her bedroom.

"And don't you need to go to work?" I asked Grant.

He chuckled and said he'd see me later.

I slept most of the day, then spent a couple hours looking at wedding venues online. LaReesa's suggestion of Vulcan Park was my favorite so far, and it wasn't too expensive, at least not to rent the venue. Reese made me dinner of some very delicious soup and a sandwich, and Grant came over before bedtime and stayed the night. I woke up in the middle of the night because my shoulder was killing me. I got out of bed and was pacing the house when Grant joined me in the living room about two a.m.

"You hurting?" he asked, after switching on a lamp.

"Yeah, a lot, actually. But I'm not due for a pill for another hour."

"I think you can go ahead and take it."

"Yeah, I might do that."

He fetched me a pill and a glass of water. I swallowed the pill and sat on the couch.

"You coming back to bed?" he asked.

"It feels better if I sit up," I answered. "You can go on. I'll sit here for a while."

He gave me a look.

"Really, I'll be fine as soon as this kicks in."

"You sure?"

"I'm sure."

A thump and a groan outside startled us both. "What was that?" I asked.

"Did you turn on the alarm?"

"I didn't."

He went back to the bedroom and returned with his gun. He opened the blinds a bit and I joined him by the window. Past the low juniper bushes in the front yard, we both saw a figure, jogging quickly down the hilly front yard toward the street. It was a man, dressed in all black, including a hoodie which covered his head and face. He got to the street and walked quickly down the block.

LaReesa's bedroom door opened and she joined us in her nightshirt. "Hey, did y'all hear—"

"Yes, there was someone outside." I said.

"Why didn't the alarm go off?" Reese asked.

"I forgot to turn it up."

Grant pulled up the camera footage on his phone. We watched as the man made his way up the yard, headed toward the bushes. The hoodie and the dark glasses he wore hid his face. I had left the sprinkler in the front yard last week, and we watched as he tripped over it, hitting the ground.

"Well, that was the thud we heard. Should we call the police?" Grant asked.

"He's gone, so what are they gonna do?"

"Good point. And I've got another one. You've been threatened, and whoever that man was may be the person who did this." He made a sweeping gesture at my shoulder. "I want you and Reese to go ahead and move in with me. Tomorrow."

"Tomorrow? Wait a minute—"

"You are moving to my house eventually anyway, right? What's wrong with now?"

"I'm injured. How am I going to move? Pack? All of that?"

"We don't have to move everything tomorrow. LaReesa and I will help you pack, but I want you somewhere where I feel it's safe."

I looked at LaReesa. "What do you think?"

"I think you need to listen to Grant. Ain't safe here."

I hated that decisions were being made for me, and I could feel my temper rising in my chest. "Look, I'm a grown woman and I can take care of myself."

Reese scoffed, "Says the woman in a sling."

"Go to bed."

"Why you mad at me? You asked what I think."

"Go. To. Bed."

LaReesa left the room in a huff and I focused on Grant. "Stop telling me what to do!"

"What's with you? I'm making decisions to keep you safe. Someone tried to kill you, you know."

"I know. I can feel it. I hate it when people make decisions for me. I feel—" I paused, assessing what I felt. "Out of control." I muttered.

Grant slid his long arms around me in a gentle hug, and that started the tears that slowly ran down my cheeks. "And scared, I would imagine."

I rested my wet cheek on his bare chest. "Yeah, some of that, too."

"That's why I want you to come live with me. Because I love you, and I want to keep you safe."

"Do you really think you can?"

"I'd die trying."

The pill kicked in and I went back to bed with Grant. I woke up the next morning late, squinting at the clock that read ten-fifteen. I got out of bed and went in search of Grant, and another pain pill.

I found him and Reese in the kitchen. Moving boxes had appeared from somewhere, and Reese was standing on the countertop, barefoot, reaching back into a high kitchen cabinet and pulling old coffee cups out of it.

"Well, good morning!" Grant said.

"You're being productive." I muttered. "Is there coffee?"

"Go sit down and I'll bring you a cup and a pill."

I went into the living room and noted there was a large U-haul rental truck parked outside. My dining room table was gone, as were the end tables in the living room. I took a deep breath as Reese brought me a pill and some coffee. I swallowed both.

"You doing okay?" she asked.

"Yeah, I'll be alright."

Grant walked in with a large box in his arms. "You okay?" he asked.

"I'm fine. I need some help getting cleaned up and dressed, then we can pack clothes."

"Okay." He took the box to the truck.

Reese said, "I gotta go pack my clothes. Grant says I can have the downstairs bedroom, with the private bath. I'm so excited!"

At least someone was.

I took a long bath in shallow water, then rested most of the day. I made a few phone calls about work. Russell was covering my cases and any new investigations I had, and I knew I owed him big-time. I called to thank him.

"You'd do the same for me."

"I would. You know I would."

Grant and Reese finished packing for the day at about four o'clock. Reese had thrown her clothes into a big box, on the hangers, without folding them or anything. It was her stuff, I thought, and her problem if they were wrinkled. Grant helped me pack my clothes, but I couldn't do much with one arm. Then he helped me into the truck. His van was at the U-haul place and he would pick it up when he turned the truck in tomorrow. He said Mamik was coming over tomorrow to help him load the rest of the heavy furniture.

The ride to the new neighborhood didn't take long at all. Grant settled me on the folding chair in the living room as he and Reese brought boxes in. I managed to unpack some of the kitchen dishes as they finished. The kitchen had a lot of cabinet space, which was nice.

"You okay?" Grant asked.

"You need a lot more furniture."

"We. We need a lot more furniture."

"Right."

"Like what?"

"We need a table for the kitchen, for one." I said.

"Won't yours work?"

"That's too big, and it will go in the dining room, no?"

"Find something you like, then. What else?"

I thought. "One of the bedrooms upstairs will be my office, right? What about your office? Will that be the other bedroom?"

"My office is the large room downstairs."

"What about a guest room?"

We decided to move my bed, the queen-sized one, into one of the rooms upstairs and use it for a guest bed. We'd use his bed for ours, along with my bedroom furniture until we could buy a new set. I ordered a new comforter set for the king-sized bed. After discussing the plans for the house with him, I realized I was enjoying planning our home together.

Maybe this marriage thing wouldn't be so bad.

Chapter Thirty-One

Mamik and Grant moved the rest of my furniture to the house the next day, Friday, with remarkable efficiency. Before I knew it, I was pointing to parts of the house where my, I mean our, stuff would go. We put my couch and chairs upstairs, temporarily, until the new furniture arrived. Reese was unpacking her stuff in her new bedroom, downstairs. Grant set up her bed and we decided on the placement for her furniture. By three o'clock, I needed a nap.

Grant woke me up about six and fed me dinner and then I went back to bed. I had a lot of stuff to do, I realized. I needed to let the school system know our new address. I needed to forward my mail. I started a list before I fell asleep.

Friday, I got a lot on the list done. I could forward the mail online, as well as update the school system. I checked in with work and everything was going well there. LaReesa stayed home from Dad's so she could help me, and she and I talked about her birthday party.

"Shall we do some sort of theme?" I asked.

"I'm not frickin' five!"

"Well, what do you want to do, then?"

"Can I have a movie party?"

"What does that entail?"

"We rent some movies and my friends come over. We could order pizza, and make popcorn."

"How many friends are we talking?"

"Sharonda, o'course, and Ella. There's another girl, Addison, who's a friend from school. I could ask her, too. Can we sleep in the living room? In sleeping bags?"

My television was now in Grant's living room. The room was plenty big enough to hold four girls. "Go ask Grant," I said.

She returned to my room from downstairs with a big smile. "He said he's cool with it. Can we get a cake?"

"Sure."

Her expression turned somber all of a sudden. "What?" I asked.

"I've never had a birthday cake."

"Really? Your grandmother never ordered you one? Or made you one?"

"Naw. I was lucky if I got a card."

"Well, we will fix that. What flavor do you want?"

"Strawberry? With cream cheese icing?"

"Sounds yummy."

Her gap-toothed smile went wide. "Thanks!"

By Monday morning, Grant and I had done everything we needed to do with the house for the moment. I had ordered a kitchen table and picked out a pretty green color for the kitchen walls. Grant went to work for a couple of hours, leaving me and Reese at home alone. The home health nurse came and changed my bandages and said my wounds looked fine, no sign of infection and they'd see me Wednesday. Dad came by to check on me and chatted with us for a while. Reese excitedly told him all the plans for her birthday. It made me happy to see her so happy.

Grant came home with a brand-new TV for the living room. It was huge. Sixty-five inches, he said.

"Wow! Really?" Reese exclaimed as they hauled it up the stairs.

"Well, I figured for a movie party, we needed a better setup."

"Awesome! This is so cool!"

Grant and Reese spent the rest of the afternoon setting the TV up in the corner of the living room. Grant had come home with a short TV table as well, with slots to hold the cable box and his TiVo. It was a smart TV, of course, with buttons for just about everything. Grant and I went to bed that night as Reese was still exploring all the features.

I propped myself up on four pillows and lay on my left side. That was the only position that was comfortable to sleep, even on the pills. Once settled, I asked, "Hey, can I ask you about something?"

Grant rolled over and faced me. "Sure."

"I'm worried about the cost of that TV. I mean, you just bought a house, and you're talking about getting a ring, and—"

He leaned over and planted a sweet kiss on my lips. "Nothing to worry about."

"Okay," I said, the doubt in my voice audible.

"I am more than fine, financially. High Tech is doing really well, and I no longer have to pay the lawyers for the trial against Regina. And the TV was on sale for four hundred bucks. We are really okay."

"Are we going to share a bank account, when we get married?"

"You haven't said you'll marry me yet."

"You haven't asked me."

"Do you want to share an account? Some couples do, some don't. I think sharing would be easier, but if you don't, that's okay."

"No, I'm fine with it, once we are married."

"Are you going to change your name?"

I tried it on for size. "Claire Summerville. Mrs. Claire Summerville. Yeah, I like it."

He kissed me again, more passionately. "I do, too."

"One more thing. My old television, did you have plans for it?"

"That tiny thing?"

"Hey, it's forty-two inches! That's not too bad."

"I thought about putting it downstairs, for Reese."

"I'd rather not. When school starts, she needs to sleep downstairs. And do homework. Her having her phone on her constantly is distracting enough."

"What did you have in mind?"

"I was thinking about giving it to Dylan and his family. His grandmother has one TV, a small one, in her bedroom. He'd like one to watch and game on, I'm sure."

I got another kiss for that statement. "That's sweet."

"Can we take it to him? Tomorrow? I want to check and see how he is doing, anyway."

"I think I have a clear afternoon, so yeah."

By Tuesday morning, I'd cut the number of pain pills I was taking in half, and wasn't miserably in pain all the time. I still had to stay in the sling due to the fractured scapula, though, for several more weeks. My car insurance company called to state they had mailed me a check for the damage to my car. Due to its age, they said, it wasn't a lot of money. I was grateful for anything.

I called Heather Maynard and told her I had a gift for her and Ryan and Dylan. I explained that Grant and I had bought a new TV and I wanted her to have my old one. She said they'd be grateful, and I told her we'd bring it to her that afternoon around three. Reese wanted to go see Dylan with us, since she was bored. We loaded up in the van. There were two boxes in the back of the van, next to the TV, that weren't there before. I asked Grant what they were.

"I have an old Xbox that I don't play anymore, and I thought I'd see if Dylan wanted it. It's pretty old, so he may not, but I thought I'd ask. The games are in the second box."

"Thanks, that's really sweet."

Reese asked if we could stop by the dollar store on the way out of town and get a couple of toys for Dylan, and I thought that sounded like a great idea. She picked out several packs of Hot Wheels toy cars and an animal coloring book and some crayons. I paid for it and we got on the interstate and headed north.

We got to the Maynards a little after three, as scheduled. When we arrived, Ryan and Dylan were outside with a man I recognized as Ryan's boss, Joe Armstrong. They were working on the old camper that stood in the Maynard's yard. It was hooked up to a large, maroon pick-up truck and they were in the process of inflating the tires on it.

We greeted them with a hello. Ryan called to Dylan, who was playing with a rock under a tree and he joined us. Reese held out the bag of toys from the dollar store.

"I got you a few toys to play with, an' a colorin' book."

Dylan said, "Thanks!" with a big smile. He and Reese went back over to the tree and I could see them opening the toys and looking at the book.

"How is he doing, Ryan?" I asked.

"He done started goin' to the counselin' and he ain't havin' as many nightmares."

"Well, that's good news."

"Heather's in the house if you wanna say hi. I gotta help Mr. Armstrong with this camper."

"Sure, I'll go find her."

We walked to the house and I knocked on the screen door. Heather opened it, dressed in a pair of old gray running shorts and a t-shirt. Her brown hair was up in a ponytail. "Hey," she said.

"Gonna be another hot day," Grant said. "We brought the TV. Let me go see if Ryan can help me bring it in." He left to go talk to Ryan and Heather asked me to come in the house.

When I entered, I could see she'd set up an old end table against the long wall next to the front door, next to a small window, across from the couch. There was an electrical outlet next to it.

"What's Ryan doing with the camper?" I asked.

"Oh! Mr. Armstrong done bought it."

"Oh, good. That'll be a little extra income, no?"

"Yeah." She lowered her voice to a near whisper. "He's gonna move it up to the farmland. He gonna live in it, too. His wife done kicked him out."

Chapter Thirty-Two

"I'm sorry to hear that," I said.

"They done been married for over twenty-five years, so I guess it can happen to anybody."

"How is Dylan doing?"

"His nightmares's a little better, and he seein' that counselor two times a week. What happened to your arm?"

"Somebody bombed my car last Monday. Killed one of my coworkers."

"Do you know who done it?"

"No, the police are working on it."

"Speakin' of the police, I ain't heard nothing from that Detective in a while. I wonder if they gonna catch who kilt my daughter."

"I'll call him this afternoon and call you with an update, okay?"

She nodded as Grant and Ryan carried the television in and placed it on the table. Dylan was hopping around excitedly as he looked at it. Reese was smiling as she watched him. Grant said he'd be right back and went to get the boxes out of the van. He brought them in and asked Dylan to join him on the couch.

Dylan sat as Grant opened the first box. "See, this is an Xbox. It's an older one, but it will work with this TV and I brought some games, too." He opened the second box. "This one was one of my favorites." He held up a case for a game that had some kind of wave runner on it. "The games are a little old, but I think they are still fun."

"Thank you!" Dylan exclaimed.

"Yeah, this's really nice of you." Heather echoed.

We watched as Dylan sorted through the games, and pulled out one. Star Wars: Knights of the Old Republic was printed on the package. "I've heard of this one." Dylan said.

"That's a good one."

"And a racing game! Cool!"

We watched as Grant hooked up the system to the television and turned it on. Dylan chose the wave runner game, which was called Wipeout, and he and Grant played a level. Dylan had a big smile on his face when he won.

We said goodbye to the Maynards and headed home. In the car, Reese talked about how happy Dylan was to get the cars, and said she was glad he got an Xbox.

"What do you want for your birthday?" I asked.

"I thought the TV was my present."

"We want to get you a couple of little things, too." Grant said.

"And a cake? And all the school clothes? I don't know what else I want, really."

Something made me suspect she'd come up with some ideas.

It was close to five when we got home, and I was due for a pill. I took one, then called Detective Graves.

"All of the clients of Mr. Summerville's have rock-solid alibis," he said after greeting me. "And they have been taken off the suspect list for Ms. Maynard's murder."

"I'm glad to hear that, and Grant will be, too."

"I've looked in to some of the people in Ms. Maynard's past, too. You mentioned the two restaurant owners, the Maples?"

"Yeah, what about them?"

"Guess who was in the EOD in the army?"

"What's EOD?"

"Explosive Ordinance Division."

"Who?"

"Caleb Maple."

"Their son?"

"Yep. Did two tours in Afghanistan, back in the nineties. I've called Birmingham Police about this. I don't know if anything will come of it, but it needs to be looked into. Other than that, I'm out of ideas."

"Thanks for the update."

I called Heather and told her that there were no updates in the investigation. I hung up with her, and went to find Grant downstairs in his office. "Hey, I just talked to Detective Graves, and he's cleared all your clients in the murder of Regina Maynard."

"Yeah, well, I could have told him that. What would be their motive? Theft of a couple hundred dollars? I can't see killing someone over that."

"You'd be surprised. The State got custody of a kid one time because his father had been shot to death over a dice game."

"Jesus. Some people, right? How does your shoulder feel?"

"I just took a pill, so it's getting better."

"What's up tomorrow? I've got a light day, so I thought we might go car shopping."

"Okay."

"You sound less than enthusiastic."

"I hate car shopping. And it's another expense."

"But think of how nice it will be to have something new."

"Or at least new-to-me."

"Nope. We are getting you a new one. You are in your car all the time for work and I want you to have something safe. I can afford it, and you are worth it."

Wednesday morning, Grant and I dropped Reese off at Dad's. She was annoyed, to say the least, that she couldn't join us on this adventure. We went to the Honda dealership in Hoover and I told Grant I wanted another Civic.

"Don't you want a grown-up car? You are over thirty, and have a child."

I laughed. "Like a minivan? No, thanks."

"I was thinking more like an SUV."

"They are too big. I like small cars."

"They have small SUVs."

We looked for a while and I test drove an H-RV that I really liked. We picked one out that was a pretty blue color with a black leather interior. The dealership would have it ready for us Friday. I held my breath as Grant wrote the check for the down payment and I did the math in my head about the monthly payments.

"It's fine," he said to me. "Would you feel better if we combined our accounts now?"

"No, no. We need to wait until we are married, but I feel

like—"

"What?'

"Like this is a one-sided relationship, financially. You make a lot more than I do."

"Ha! I'm your sugar daddy."

"Really, I'm serious."

He leaned over and kissed my forehead. "Stop worrying."

Easier said than done, I thought. We headed for the door of the dealership when I spotted someone quickly climbing into an older maroon Toyota Tacoma truck near the exit. The salesperson he had been talking to looked very confused as he sped out of the parking lot.

"What?" Grant asked.

"I could have sworn I just saw—"

"Who?"

"Mr. Armstrong. Joe Armstrong."

Chapter Thirty-Three

"Ryan Maynard's boss?"

"Yeah."

"That's weird."

"Right? Why would he be here? He's living in that used camper because his wife kicked him out. He can't afford a new car right now. Why is he following us?"

"We don't know that he is."

I shot him a look. "Of course he is. I want to go talk to him and find out what's up."

"No! You're already badly injured. We have a follow-up with your surgeon today, and then we need to get home so you can rest. Then I need to go clean your old house so we can get it on the market."

Grant drove us to the surgeon's office downtown, near the UAB hospital where I had been. He checked everything and said it looked like it was healing nicely. He re-prescribed the antibiotics, ordered another x-ray of my scapula, which we had done. He said he would call me with the results. It was close to five when we finished, and we got to Dad's at almost six o'clock, due to the rush-hour traffic.

Dad and Reese were watching TV in his den when we arrived to pick her up. "You get a car?" She asked, excitement in her voice.

"I did. I bought an H-RV. I pick it up Friday."

"What's that?"

"It's kinda like a smaller version of a C-RV."

"Cool!"

"Everything good here?"

"Yeah, we've just been hanging out." Dad said.

We got Reese in the van and headed home. On the way, Grant answered a call from a woman named Susie, who had been a client of his in the past. She was a real estate agent and we made an appointment to meet at my old house late tomorrow morning, Thursday, so she could look at it and list it. I was quiet after that call.

"You okay?" Grant asked.

"Yeah, it's just a little sad to be selling my house. I've

only had it a couple of years, and I like that place."

"But on to bigger and better things, yeah?"

I smiled. "True."

Grant asked Reese if she would be willing to go to my old house with us tomorrow morning, and earn little money helping to clean it up. She agreed, and Thursday the three of us got to the house at about nine. I was limited as to what I could do with one arm, but after we unloaded the bucket of cleaning supplies, I managed to scrub the kitchen counters with my left hand. Reese vacuumed while I skootched around on my butt on the floor and dusted the baseboards. It was weird to see the house empty.

Susie arrived and inspected the house. We went over everything, decided on a list price, and signed the contract. The for-sale sign would go up tomorrow, and Susie was optimistic it would sell quickly.

I sighed, fighting back tears. Everything was happening quickly.

Friday morning, we picked up my new car from the Honda dealership. I loved the smell of the new leather interior and it was very comfortable to drive. Getting it in gear with my left hand was the most uncomfortable part of driving it.

"How do you like it?" Grant asked.

"I love it. It's so spacious after my little Civic."

I turned from Highway 31 onto the onramp for I-459, heading south on the interstate bypass toward our neighborhood. I couldn't help but notice there was a truck following us. It was a maroon Toyota, like I'd seen Joe Armstrong speeding away in from the dealership.

"You see that truck behind us?" I asked.

He turned in his seat and looked. "Yeah, what about it?"

"I think that's Joe Armstrong."

"What?"

"That's the truck that he sped out of the dealership in on Wednesday."

"Claire, there are about a million burgundy trucks in Alabama."

"That's true, I guess."

But my sixth sense was telling me to pay attention.

I was in the right lane, going the speed limit of seventy miles an hour. The truck, now about two car lengths behind me, changed lanes. He was now on my left and speeding up. Exit 10 was coming up, and I had the intention of getting off there, and taking Highway 150 home.

The truck sped quickly up on my left side. I glanced to the left and could see the driver looking at me, a man, in a baseball cap and mirrored aviator sunglasses.

He suddenly swiped my way. The proximity alarm on the car beeped loudly and an orange "BRAKE" flashed on the instrument panel. I jerked the wheel to the right and he just missed my left front quarter panel as he sped off. My car went off the interstate and over the rough shoulder as I slammed on the brakes. We skid into the grass on the side of the road as we stopped, nearly missing the ditch and the trees on the other side of it.

"What the hell!" I screamed.

"Are you okay?"

The sudden stop had jerked my shoulder a bit, and it hurt. "I tweaked my shoulder, but I'm all right. You okay? Did you get the license number?"

"I'm okay, and I didn't."

I noticed I was shaking. "Dammit. I've had this car ten freaking minutes. Can you drive the rest of the way?"

Grant agreed and we got out and inspected the car as we switched seats. There wasn't any damage, other than grass clippings all around the wheel well and the smell of overheated brakes.

"What the hell was he doing?" I asked to no one in particular.

"Trying to kill you, obviously."

"Why?"

"Good question."

"I'm going up there to talk to him."

"No."

"Yes."

"Then I'm going with you. If you are going to be stupid, I guess we're going to be stupid together."

We were nearly to Blount County when I realized I had no idea where I was going. I Googled "Armstrong Farms" on my cell phone and was taken to their location on Maps. The farm itself was on County Road 8, in Cullman County, north of where the Maynards lived. We exited the interstate and followed the Maps directions until we came to an enormous peach farm. Rows of squat peach trees were planted perpendicular to the highway and seemed to reach out into the horizon for miles toward the hills. The trees were green and leafy, and on a few of them, I could see plump peaches that had not been picked.

We drove through the gates, the trees now fenced in on either side of us by a low, wooden fence. I could see an orange tractor parked on one of the red dirt pathways that separated the trees. We drove for a quarter mile or so and arrived at a big red barn that sat in a clearing in the trees. The Maynards old camper was parked to the side of it.

Grant stopped the car. "Now what?"

"I have no idea. I don't really have a plan. I think I will go knock on the door."

I exited the H-RV, wincing as my shoulder complained. I was due for a pill, come to think of it. Grant followed me to the door of the camper and I knocked. I looked around for the maroon truck and didn't see it.

"Not home." Grant said.

"Apparently."

"I'm going to go look in the barn."

The red barn door rolled up like a garage's, and it was open. I peeked in to see more farm equipment, including lots of attachments for the orange tractor. I could see an auger and a pesticide sprayer.

"He's not here, either!" I called out to Grant. There was an office built into the back part of the barn, and the door was wide open with the fluorescent lights on. I headed there. Grant was outside and didn't follow me. "I'll be right back!"

I made my way to the office, which held a large, very crowded desk that faced a worn, black leather couch against the wall to the left. I stood in front of the desk and surveyed what was on there. I saw a checkbook and a desktop computer, along with other office supplies and papers. The computer was on, but the monitor showed a moving screen saver. I bumped the mouse on the desk to see what would happen.

A security screen appeared, asking for name and password. So much for that. To the left of the monitor, I saw a letter from an attorney. I glanced at it, and saw that a Mr. Jonathan Culligan had been retained by Mrs. Diane Armstrong to represent her in her divorce from Joe Armstrong. I reached for it as I heard a "click-click".

I looked up to see Joe Armstrong in front of me, holding a rifle.

"What the hell do you think you're doing?" he yelled.

The noise had startled me, and my shoulder complained again, so I winced. I answered his question with another question. "What were you doing running us off the road earlier?"

"You just can't mind your business, can you? You won't leave nothing alone."

"You didn't answer my question."

"She was suing me! Suing me for child support!" he screamed. I saw the barrel of the gun waving around and prayed he wouldn't pull the trigger.

"Child support? Are you Dylan's father?" I suddenly realized Dylan and Joe had the same eye shape, and color.

"She seduced me! That young slut! She came to work with her father during her Spring Break and seduced me! Right there on that couch!"

"I ran Dylan's name through our records and didn't see any pending court action."

"Did you check Cullman County?"

I hadn't.

"You didn't, did you? If you had just left it alone, no one else would have died. You did this. You caused that other girl to die! And you caused my wife to leave me! They sent a notice about the court action! She found out about the kid! She found out I was seduced!"

"No—"

"And now you have to die." He sighted the gun at me again.

"Wait—"

A sudden loud clanging noise behind Joe caused him to glance around briefly. I could see Grant there, who had knocked something metal off one of the farm instruments onto the concrete floor.

"You! Get over here!" Joe shouted, turning the gun on him.

Grant joined me in front of the desk. "You okay?" he whispered.

I nodded, subtly, and said, "Mr. Armstrong is Dylan's father. Regina was suing him for child support."

"I heard."

"He says it's my fault that Sydney died. Because I wouldn't leave it alone."

"You were just doing your job."

"Enough talking!" Joe shouted.

"Joe, the police are going to figure out that it's you." I said. "You're leaving a trail of bodies behind you."

"I am going to burn this place to the ground. All of it. They might find your bones."

I glanced up at Grant's face. Flashes of what would have been our wedding went through my mind. A white dress. Little purple flowers. I stopped myself from focusing on that. Grant looked down at me, then his gaze drifted to his pants. I could see a hard lump in his right pocket. He had his gun on him. If he could get it out...

I took one step forward, putting myself between Joe and Grant. "But what about your employees? None of this is Ryan Maynard's fault. He had no idea that his daughter was sleeping around with so many men. You are going to leave him without the only job he's had since he was a teenager. How is he going to support little Dylan?"

"That's not my problem!"

I sensed Grant move and knew he was slipping his hand into his pocket.

"And don't you want a relationship with your son? Dylan is a great kid, very smart. He could take over the farm one day."

Joe was thinking about that, I could see. I felt Grant move

210

again. I kept talking.

"Do you have any other children, Joe?"

"No! My wife couldn't have children, and we are way too old to raise one now. Enough talking!" His finger moved to the trigger.

Grant stepped forward and shoved me to the left. I stumbled, nearly falling to the ground, just as a loud bang echoed in the room.

I let out an involuntary, short scream.

Joe Armstrong looked surprised.

Blood began to spread across his shirt, on his upper abdomen. He dropped the gun. His hands went to the wound. He fell onto the floor, onto his back, groaning in pain.

I looked up to see Detective Graves standing there, his gun in hand.

Chapter Thirty-Four

The loud bang, I realized, had come from Detective Graves's gun, not Grant's. I looked at Grant, seeing the relief on his face. Three uniformed Sheriff's officers appeared from somewhere. They held their guns toward Joe Armstrong as he groaned on the floor. One picked up the rifle. Detective Graves was on his radio, requesting an ambulance.

Grant put his gun back in his pocket and his arms went around me. I sank into his chest as Joe Armstrong moaned on the floor.

I stood back from Grant and thanked the detective. "How did you get here?"

"Mr. Summerville texted me earlier. Said you'd been having some sort of trouble with Joe Armstrong and he figured you would wind up here."

"He's little Dylan's father, and Regina Maynard was suing him for child support. His wife found out and was leaving him."

"Why come after you?"

"It's my job to investigate who Dylan's father is. To be honest, I would have never guessed him. If he had just laid low, he wouldn't have been discovered."

Joe Armstrong had lost consciousness, and there was a huge pool of blood around him. "I'm not sure he is going to make it," Graves said. He asked an officer to put pressure on the wound. The cop knelt and did so. Joe's breathing was shallow and his color was gray.

"Let's step outside," The detective said.

Sirens were wailing all around outside and within moments, many more Blount County Sheriff's Department officers arrived. Detective Graves updated everybody, and a supervisor was called. The officer who had been pressuring Joe Armstrong's wound walked out of the barn, blood all over his tan uniform, and shook his head slowly at the Detective.

The ambulance arrived from the Fire Department a few minutes later and Joe Armstrong was declared dead. The Detective surrendered his weapon to the Supervisor in charge, and Grant and I were interviewed separately, and it took a while to tell the whole story. I called Dad and gave him a quick update and said I'd be home as soon as I could.

Grant and I finally got back to Hoover at about eight o'clock at night. We picked up LaReesa, who was full of questions about why we were late. We told her an abbreviated version on the way home. Reese made us some sandwiches as we sat in silence on the couch after we got home. I finally took a pain pill. My shoulder was killing me.

"Are you okay?" I asked Grant. "This is the first time you've seen someone killed, and I'm worried about you."

"I'm just glad Detective Graves showed up when he did, to be honest. I was just about to shoot him."

"I'm glad you didn't have to."

We slept very late the next day, Saturday. On Monday, I went back to work. Sydney's extended family lived in Tennessee and her funeral was that day. Mac had gone up there for it, and I was grateful he did.

The news covered the officer-involved shooting without too many details. The next week, Detective Graves called me. The investigation was completed, he said, and his shooting of Joe Armstrong had been deemed justified. Regina Maynard's case was closed.

I went to Heather and Ryan's house on Tuesday to talk about everything that had happened. Diane Armstrong was Joe's wife, and his heir, since they were not divorced yet at the time of his death. She had called Ryan Saturday to talk to him about the farm. She wanted to hire him to manage it, with a pay increase, if he was willing.

"That's great news!" I said.

He gave a sheepish nod. "I'll handle all the farm work, and she'll do the accounting and the payroll and stuff. Says she's gonna make sure we get paid on time, in the future."

"Where's Dylan?"

"He's outside playing somewhere."

"Joe Armstrong was his father."

Heather and Ryan shared a look. Ryan said, "We knew she was—having sex—in high school. We didn't know it was with my boss."

Heather asked, "Do you think she were like that because

214

my Daddy touched her?"

"Sexually abused kids do tend to act out that way, sometimes. But there are a lot of other reasons they do, too. Attention, or control. I don't think there was any way you could have prevented it."

"Should we tell Dylan who his daddy was?" Heather asked.

"Honestly, that's up to you. I think he is too young to understand much, now. He may have questions as he gets older."

"I think we'll wait till he has questions."

"I think that's a good choice."

The Maynards went to court the next week and were granted custody of Dylan. I transferred his case to Blount County for a time of supervision until things got settled. The Maynards mailed me a photograph of Dylan six months later. It was his second-grade school picture, and he had lost most of his front teeth. I could see that because of his wide smile.

On the evening of July 29, my living room was filled with four giggling, shrieking girls. Grant had bought four air mattresses that supported sleeping bags in the living room. One of the mattresses had a loose valve and when you moved on it, it made a farting noise. Hence all the giggling and shrieking.

Dad came over and we retreated to the side porch, drinks in hand, and left the girls to it.

"They sure are acting silly in there." Grant said.

"They are acting like kids and having fun," I answered. "Nothing wrong with that."

Grant put his Fat Tire down on the black metal side table and stood up. He glanced at Dad. "Well, I guess it's time."

"Time for what?" I asked.

Grant got down on one knee. He pulled a small box out of his pocket. My heart raced as I took a deep breath.

He opened the box. "Will you marry me?"

I glanced at Dad, who had a big smile on his face. I was filled with only emotions of excitement, and happiness. "Yes!"

Inside the box was a beautifully cut Marquise diamond on a gold band. He slid it onto my left ring finger, a big smile on his face. Then he kissed me.

"Did you know about this?" I asked Dad.

"Oh, we've been talking for weeks. You have my wholehearted support. We'll talk budget later."

I laughed. "I guess we should go tell our daughter."

Grant stuck his head through the French doors to the living room and asked Reese to step outside. She did, and asked "What's up?"

I held out my left hand and she screamed in excitement, which led to three other girls joining us on the porch.

"'Bout damn time!" Reese exclaimed.

We went back in the house and all the girls fawned over the ring and congratulated us. Reese wanted to know if I'd decided on a location, and a color, and a dress, and I finally threw up my hands and asked for a break. "We have plenty of time to decide all this."

The doorbell rang. "That'll be the pizza," I said, and walked down the half-flight of stairs to the front door.

It wasn't the pizza. Tori O'Leary stood there with a Birmingham police officer.

"Hi Tori. What's up?" I asked.

"Is LaReesa home?"

"She is. It's her birthday, and she's having a slumber party." I noticed it had gone quiet upstairs, and all the girls could hear everything. "What's going on?"

"I'm sorry for the bad news, but LaReesa's mother was found deceased this afternoon."

THE END

216

Turn the page to read about the other books in the
Social worker Claire Conover Mystery Series

Little Lamb Lost

Social worker Claire Conover honestly believed she could make a difference in the world until she got the phone call she's dreaded her entire career. One of her young clients, Michael, has been found dead, and his mother, Ashley, has been arrested for his murder. And who made the decision to return Michael to Ashley? Claire Conover.

Ashley had seemingly done everything right - gotten clean, found a place to live, worked two jobs, and earned back custody of her son. Devastated but determined to discover where her instincts failed her, Claire vows to find the truth about what really happened to Michael.

What Claire finds is no shortage of suspects. Ashley's boyfriend made no secret that he didn't want children. And Ashley's stepfather, an alcoholic and a chronic gambler, has a shady past. And what about Michael's mysterious father and his family? Or Ashley herself? Was she really using again?

Amidst a heap of unanswered questions, one thing is for certain: Claire Conover is about to uncover secrets that could ruin lives - or end her own.

Little Girl Gone

Claire Conover is back in the sequel to *Little Lamb Lost*. She has taken a 13-year-old girl into custody after she is found sleeping behind a grocery store. The girl's murdered mother is found at a construction site owned by a family friend, then the girl disappears. Her mother worked in an illegal gambling industry in Birmingham. Things only get more complicated from there. Is it possible the girl pulled the trigger? She doesn't have a lot of street smarts, so where could she have run? Claire has to find the answers, and the girl, fast.

Little White Lies

Claire Conover is drawn into another mystery when the office of black mayoral candidate Dr. Marcus Freedman is bombed. Marcus is found safe, but his campaign manager Jason O'Dell is found dead in the rubble. Claire's office gets a call about Jason's daughter who was left at her daycare, and she becomes Claire's latest charge. Further investigation reveals that Jason was living under an assumed name, and is really Jason Alsbrook, son of prominent local mine owner James Alsbrook. James holds many records in Alabama, including the most accidents and deaths in his mines. Any number of people would wish harm to him or his family. Claire works to keep little Maddie safe as she faces new challenges in her relationship with computer programmer Grant Summerville. She investigates Jason's death with the help of her friend and reporter Kirk Mahoney, and they become closer. The addition of a foster child further complicates everything as she must make some decisions about her future with Grant.